Prue's body smelled of some intoxicating fragrance that Keeley didn't recognize. She felt so soft against Keeley's side with her arm lying across Keeley's chest and her knee resting over Keeley's thigh. It made Keeley ask herself why lying next to Prue would be wrong. Keeley wasn't Attie's husband or anything like that . . .

"Then may I kiss you?"

Kiss me? But Keeley made no effort to stop her. Prue's mouth was softer than Attie's, and larger. Attie used her tongue, but not much. Right now, Prue was all over the inside of Keeley's mouth. And then here came Prue's hand beneath Keeley's gown. Keeley forgot all about her worries as Prue slowly worked Keeley's gown above her breasts before caressing Keeley's skin from shoulder to knee. Keeley could only manage to breathe. She felt her body relax and her bones melt into the mattress. Prue sat up and removed her own nightgown. She pulled Keeley's from her, then lay full-length on top of her.

Keeley slid her arms around Prue and held her tightly as Prue nestled between Keeley's thighs. She began to play with Keeley's nipples using her lips and tongue, pulling on Keeley and caressing her with long damp strokes across each breast.

Keeley felt heat building within her. She was going to leap right off this bed if Prue did one more little thing to her. And then Prue did, gently taking Keeley's hardened nipple between her teeth and tugging on it, just a little. Keeley felt herself start to go.

LOOKING FOR NAIAD?

Buy our books at
www.naiadpress.com

or call our toll-free number
1-800-533-1973

or by fax (24 hours a day)
1-850-539-9731

Omaha's BELL

BY
PENNY HAYES

THE NAIAD PRESS, INC.
1999

Printed in the United States of America on acid-free paper
First Edition

Editor: Christine Cassidy
Cover designer: Bonnie Liss (Phoenix Graphics)
Typesetter: Sandi Stancil

Library of Congress Cataloging-in-Publication Data

Hayes, Penny, 1940 –
    Omaha's bell / by Penny Hayes.
        p.   cm.
    ISBN 1-56280-232-1   (alk. paper)
    I. Title.
PS3558.A835046   1999
813'.54—dc21
                                                          98-44751
                                                            CIP

To Crystal

About the Author

Penny Hayes was born in Johnson City, New York, February 1940. As a child she lived on a farm near Binghamton, New York. She later attended college in Utica, Buffalo and Huntington, WV, graduating with degrees in art and in elementary and special education. She has made her living teaching in both New York State and southern West Virginia. She presently resides in central New York. Ms. Hayes' interests include backpacking, mountain climbing, canoeing, traveling, reading and gardening. She recently retired from teaching and is now writing full time. She has been published in *I Know You Know,* and *Of the Summits and of the Forests* and various backpacking magazines. Her novels include *The Long Trail, Yellowthroat, Montana Feathers, Grassy Flats, Kathleen O'Donald, Now and Then* and *City Lights/Country Candles. Omaha's Bell* is her eighth novel. She has also written short stories for *The Erotic Naiad* ("Flowers"), *The Romantic Naiad* ("Chinese Dinner"), *The Mysterious Naiad* ("Grandma"), *The First Time Ever* ("One Detail Glaringly Lacking"), *Dancing in the Dark* ("A Little Time") and *Lady Be Good* ("Haunted").

Chapter One

The rider charged down the sandy slope at a dead run, her mustang's white-and-tan-spotted coat plastered with foamy lather. The horse's lithe body moved with rapid, smooth rhythm, making short work of the earth beneath him until the road dropped sharply and he slid to a near stop. His hooves kicked up eruptions of small rocks and billowing dust as he sat on his haunches to slide down the steep terrain. Thunder rolled low and deep like the rumbling wheels of a train heard from a long way off, steadily drawing closer and closer. In the last half-hour, the sky had

1

turned gun-metal gray, growing darker by the minute. Lightning illuminated the stark silhouette of the horse's desperate passenger as she was carried down the steep hill.

Keeley Delaney felt the pinto begin to topple to his right. She threw all her weight to her left and prayed he'd recover. She felt him straighten himself, then she dug her roweled spurs into his sides, pushing him hard and harder still as their downward plunge continued and their speed increased.

She clutched the horn to keep from being thrown from the saddle as the horse hit the flat prairie in a skid, still on his rump. There, he came to an abrupt stop. Thrust over his neck, Keeley cursed and yelled, kicking him into renewed motion. He lunged, pushing his big-muscled rear into a full-blown charge. Ready for him, she yelled, "Come on, Jingles. Hyaah!" Grit flew into her mouth. She ground the minute particles to pulp as she clenched her teeth and locked her gaze on Omaha, lying a mile and a half ahead.

They tore across the prairie, the rider spurring her mount onward, crouching low over his neck and screaming words of encouragement to him as they drove toward the finish line.

Keeley ignored the shouts and curses of riders behind her. She hadn't during last month's race, and it had cost her precious time and a fifty-dollar prize. This time the purse had been raised to a hundred dollars, and so she concentrated only on staying low in the saddle, so low that Jingles' coarse mane whipped across her face and slashed at her eyes.

The race had been a long one, five miles this time. Only her most skillful riding would win her this event. And win she *would* — and be cursed for it.

Her hat had flown from her head long ago, its chin thong stretching across her throat, the hat whipping wildly back and forth, battering itself against her back. She wore a long-sleeved, blue cotton shirt and heavy, tan canvas pants. Well-worn leather boots were rammed into the stirrups.

Thunder exploded directly overhead, frightening Jingles and triggering even greater speed from him.

"Move over, Delaney!" Hawk Blackbean had finally caught up with her. If anyone was going to beat her, it would be he and Dante, that half-wild, crazy black stallion that Blackbean, himself half horse, rode.

Blackbean was big and lean. He was as friendly as a grizzly and looked like one with his mangy black hair and beard, so long that during the race he wore both hair and beard tied out of his way with a raw-hide thong. At his current speed, his pelt flew straight back over his shoulder. Except for a large-brimmed hat pulled down low and regular boots, he was dressed in fringed deerskin darkened with stains, grease and wear.

I ain't afraid of no half-man, half-animal, and he ain't going to beat me, neither, Keeley vowed silently. *Not this time, he ain't*. He had in the last race.

She felt Jingles lose his stride when Hawk yelled, "Outta my way, Delaney!" He reached out, ruthlessly slapping Jingles' rump. She was nearly cast from the saddle as Jingles abruptly shied to the right, but she managed to hook her elbow around the horn, checking her fall as she toppled sideways. She hauled herself upright, cursing Hawk as she watched him pull ahead.

Repeatedly spurring her mount, she brought Jingles back into line and nosed him up to Dante. For a short time both horses ran neck and neck.

3

From the corner of her eye, she saw Hawk raise his hand again. As he did, she eased Jingles into Dante, attempting to force him off course, but Blackbean held the stallion firm. Wild-eyed and snorting heavily with every rapid breath, Dante obeyed his rider and pushed hard against Jingles. Keeley could feel Hawk's stirrup knocking against hers, his barrel-chested mount shoving Jingles aside with his greater weight and size. Slowly and steadily, Hawk pulled out and away from Keeley. The dirt from Dante's hooves stung her unprotected face as she hurled curses at Blackbean's back.

A wide, red paper ribbon strung across Main Street marked the finish line ahead. Another thirty seconds and the ends of the sash would be flying back from either side of Dante's thick chest, the streamers fluttering wildly along the stallion's sides. Another thirty seconds, and she could go home and not come back to town again. Not with her head held high, she couldn't. A thick crowd of men, women and children waited on either side of the street, shouting encouragement to the riders and waving their hats in the air.

"Come on, Jingles!" Keeley shouted. "Come *on*!" Even with Blackbean in front, she wouldn't give up. With mere yards to go, she yelled and slapped Jingles' haunches with the ends of her long reins. She would not look at Hawk's back, Dante's rump, the town ahead. She would just close her eyes and *ride*! And she did, trusting completely that Jingles would bring them home.

They flew across the line, the rest of the riders thundering in behind them. A thick blanket of dust reduced visibility to almost nothing, but it made no difference what she could or couldn't see. There had been just one rider too many ahead of her. And then the rains came down hard and heavy, and she could barely see ten yards before her.

Omaha's long, wide main street had been temporarily cleared of horses, wagons, buggies, horseback riders and pedestrians for the late-afternoon race. The industrious town had grown from a shaky building or two in its earliest days to a rapidly growing city. Fort Omaha was situated north of the city, along with the town's many saloons, three banks, two emporiums, several ladies' shops, a bakery, a butcher's shop, a haberdashery and three hardware and gun supply stores. Additionally, with the great Missouri River close by, supplies continuously flowed north and south. Emigrants journeyed through Omaha to points west, keeping the place stirring while its remaining populace, including countless dogs and cats, wandered its streets on business or pleasure. Private homes lined up on the town's outskirts. From there extended ranches and farms where grain and cattle were a growing source of income for Omaha.

Keeley and the remaining racers were halfway through town before they could bring their mounts to a halt. They trotted back to the finish line where several men willing to ignore the cloudburst were cheering and shooting their pistols into the air. As the contestants reached them, tall willowy Sheriff Lon Butts brought their rowdy antics to a stop with an upraised hand and a commanding voice.

Keeley approached the judge, who, dressed in black garments and a tall black hat, squinted through the rain at her. As she slid from the saddle, several rough hands caught her and dragged her the rest of the way.

5

Amongst much indistinguishable yelling and hooting, she was dumped upright onto a nearby wagonbed. She expected to be soundly taunted for having run today. She supposed she had asked for it. No woman did the things she did or lived the way she did — at least not in Nebraska territory. A few homesteaded independently, but somehow they remained ladies, wearing skirts even while working in the fields and, during good weather, driving their buggies to church each Sunday.

She waited for the attacks to subside, thinking the men would be less hard on her if she stood strong and took it instead of whining about it. She wished she understood what they were saying, but with the lightning cracking all around and the thunder exploding so loud that even little children were likely to be crying, it was impossible.

She finally made out a single coherent sentence. "Here you go, Keeley," the gruff voice said. A big mug of cold beer was shoved into her hand. She looked at it, blinking away the water pouring down her face. It was a darned cold rain for the first of May, and she began to shiver. "What's this for?" she croaked. In spite of the soggy weather, her throat was still dry as dust.

Hawk Blackbean leaned against a wagon wheel, breathing heavily, his thick chest rising and falling like a heaving cow about to calve. The rain flowing off the brim of his hat concealed his black eyes. Able to see only his long, narrow nose and thin lips, she watched his mustache rhythmically working up and down as he said, "Drink up, Delaney. You won."

"What're you talking about?" She took a big swig from the mug, not caring that he lied. Something heavy banged against her teeth. "Ugh, what was that?"

The group, some on horseback, others standing on the wooden sidewalk beneath sheltering porch roofs, howled with amusement. She poured the rest of the beer onto the ground. Bills and a few silver coins followed the golden brew and fell into a puddle of foamy mud. The men backed away from the money, breaking into greater laughter.

"Damn you, Blackbean! You did this, didn't you? You pitiful loser." She'd won! She didn't know how, but she'd won! She jumped to the ground to snatch up her prize, but Hawk beat her to it, leaving the coins but grabbing the wad of bills.

In a rage, she jumped on him, screaming, "Give me that money! It's mine!" The onlookers shouted, giving the scrappers a wide berth as she and Hawk brawled all the way across the street. She rode him like she would a bucking bronco, raking him with her spurs and clinging like a wildcat to his back. She yanked his hair until she drew back his head far enough to make him yell for mercy, which she did not give. "Give me that money, Hawk Blackbean, or I'll kill you. I mean it!" She reached impotently for the soggy bills he held at arm's length.

Their legs became entangled, and Hawk fell backward, landing on top of Keeley, driving the breath from her and half-burying her in the stinking quagmire the street had become. She was dazed but not out. Fighting to refill her lungs as white dots of light exploded before her eyes, she wrapped her arms around his throat and hung on, biting his neck through his hair, reaching around and clawing at his face and eyes.

"Hit him, Keeley! Grab her tits, Hawk!" Men goaded both fighters as Keeley's breath slowly returned.

Two shots split the air, and the ring of onlookers scattered. "What in hell's going on here? Blackbean, get up. Keeley Delaney, you get your feathers home where they belong." Sheriff Butts yanked Hawk to his feet. "You folks ain't gonna be doing this every month. I've had enough." He holstered his pistol and gave Hawk a push toward his horse. "No more races in Omaha, y'all hear? No more!"

Keeley struggled to stand as the others moved on. Foul mire and dung dripped from her body as she scraped muck from her face and wiped her hands down the front of her mud-sodden shirt. The hard rain had changed to a miserable, steady drizzle.

Tiny Johnnie White's long duster slapped around his feet as he moved. His hat was so large it bent his ears downward. White closely resembled a weasel both in looks and deed and carefully sided with whoever appeared to be coming out on top in any situation. He cackled through yellowed and broken teeth, "Come on, Blackbean. I'll buy you a drink. You done real good." He had to stretch to lay a chummy arm across Hawk's broad shoulders.

With his muddied sleeve, Hawk swiped at his nose. "Nah, White, I'll buy you one." Slime clung to his face. He turned and fanned his hand toward the rest of the men. It still clutched Keeley's winnings. "Hell, I'll buy you all one." There were a number of happy shouts, then Butts' gun went off again.

"No, you ain't, Blackbean." He pointed his weapon toward Hawk.

"Why the hell not?" Somehow Hawk's hat was still

on his head. He yanked it off and threw it to the ground. Rain rolled off his long, greasy hair. His hand slid to the handle of the Bowie knife he carried in a rattlesnake-hide sheath looped through his belt.

"Give Delaney that money."

White dropped his arm from Hawk's back and sidled away. The entire town knew of Blackbean's tinderbox temper.

Those who had decided to join Blackbean at the saloon halted, their boots sucking mud as they shifted from one foot to the other and waited for a final decision on the money. Hawk's lips tightened, disappearing beneath his moustache. Keeley watched his black eyes lock onto Butts' like a starving dog's on a meaty bone.

"Give her the money, son." Butts' gun remained pointed at Blackbean's chest. The barrel never wavered as a steady wind began to blow, brisk and chilling, inviting living creatures to find shelter very soon. Butts' brown eyes, buried below wild brown eyebrows, remained as steady as his pistol. Clean shaven, his face was heavily creased with weather lines. He was young, and he was fast with both pistol and rifle. He was also respected enough that even older men allowed him to call them "son." From his six-feet-two-inch height, he had spoken through lips that moved little more than an anchored fencepost. Still, he was always understood, and Keeley had heard his words plain as a chirping bird on a fine spring morning.

"You want it, Butts, you take it." Hawk held out the greenbacks, but his fist was tightly balled around them.

Johnnie White and the others disappeared into

saloons, stores and cafes with only a couple of die-hards remaining to watch Blackbean take a bullet, or Butts succumb to Hawk's blade. A number of wagons now clogged the roadway, their wheels sunk deep in the mud. Drays and buggies fought to move forward as oxen and mules bellowed in protest against their sorry lot. People dashed across open alleyways, quickly ducking beneath protecting porch overhangs where rain drizzled like thin waterfalls. A few wives had come along and were firmly herding several men away from the explosive and unsightly activities.

Butts cocked the hammer. "All right, son," he said to the older man. "If that's the way you want it." The gun roared, and Hawk landed on his seat.

Hawk clutched at his chest, feeling for bullet holes, his disbelieving eyes round as silver dollars. "Jesus Christ, Butts! You damn near shot me." The bills lay scattered in the street. The wind, much stronger now, blew them haphazardly across the ground.

"If I'd wanted to shoot you, Blackbean, I would have. Now you get on home too. The race is over, and there ain't gonna be any more here in Omaha. This ain't a frontier town anymore. You men need to get that through those thick heads of yours." His eyes scanned any who might be listening.

Sulking and muttering, Hawk collected his hat and rode out. Butts holstered his gun and turned on Keeley. "Delaney, pick up your winnings and get on home. You caused enough trouble around here today. You damn near got a man shot over your foolishness."

Keeley erupted. "*I* almost got him shot? I didn't do anything except try to get my money that I won fair and square." She scrambled to collect the wayward bills. As wet as they were, they flew through the air like discarded scraps. She hoped she could find all the coins she'd dumped. It was going to be a fine thing digging through mud and dung a half-foot deep to recover them all.

"Yeah, you, Keeley. You won. Dante stumbled, and you won. You got your money. Now get on home. I don't want to see you in town for a week, you got that? A week. Any sooner, and I just might throw you in jail."

"You'd put a woman in jail for coming to town?"

"That's just it, Keeley. You ain't a woman. And you ain't a man, neither. There ain't no proper protection for people like you. Men are suspicious of you, women hate you and children are afraid of you. Now get on home."

Keeley trudged over to him stuffing the last of the soggy bills into her pants pocket. "You got no call speaking to me that way, Sheriff. Plain and simple, you can't tolerate that I'm a woman, and I beat a man at a man's game."

A foot taller, he towered above her. The rain, again falling heavily, poured off his brim onto her upturned face. "Oh, I can handle it all right, Keeley. It's you who can't handle what the hell *you* are." He tipped his hat, then walked away.

She shook the cold water from her eyes. Thick, earthen ooze stunk up the air as she looked around for Jingles. Scowling and seething, she wanted to scream at Butts that he was wrong — about who she was, about how she should behave. She lived free, and she would stay free. Let others exist like caged animals hemmed in by rules. Not her! Not Keeley Delaney.

Someone had tied the gelding to a rail across the

11

street in front of the Prudence Jane Restaurant. She plodded over to him, proud of how well he'd done today. She ran her hand down his barrel, inspecting his sides. She'd nailed him solid, but a little ointment should heal his hide. She wasn't happy about that, but she'd make it up to him. There'd be a little extra grain tonight and a fine, long rubdown.

"You should take better care of him."

Keeley recognized Prudence Jane's voice. Nobody else's sounded so pure; no one spoke as properly, never saying "ain't" and "he don't." But then, Miss Morris came from Philadelphia, Pennsylvania, and they spoke real fine back there, pleasing Keeley's ears to no end.

Prudence Morris was the most beautiful woman Keeley had ever seen; she would have gone to the restaurant a lot more if she had the time and money. Sometimes when she did go, she sat on a stool at the counter and drank coffee until she had to piss so badly she couldn't stay any longer, while all the time watching Prue, listening to her talk pretty and wishing she could bring her home and keep her forever right there in Keeley's soddy and claim her like nobody's business. Yes, she'd like that, all right, and she was fairly sure that Prue would too from the way Prue looked at her and slipped her a free cookie from time to time. Things being what they were, however, it wasn't likely to happen.

"Yeah, well, we all gotta earn our keep. I'll treat him good tonight." Keeley felt a small amount of irritation as she mounted up and settled her fanny against the cantle. Her tailbone hurt, and she stood a little in the stirrups before reseating herself.

"A horse is just a poor, dumb animal, and its

owner ought to know better." Prue's fine blue cotton dress fit her small, slim body perfectly, the bodice molding seductively over her large breasts and womanly curves. Her long, blond hair was piled neatly upon her head. She wore a white wool shawl around her shoulders. Her mouth was rouged, and when she smiled the color made her even teeth stand out whiter than they were. She frowned at Keeley, her blue eyes slightly admonishing.

Keeley scratched behind her ear with mud-packed nails, her mouth tightening. Unable to think of anything pleasant to say, she clucked to Jingles, pointed him toward the north end of town and rode out.

If it cleared off and warmed up enough, she'd take time this evening to sit for a while in the creek by the barn before she went to bed. That would make her feel better. What wasn't making her feel better was knowing that Prue's eyes were boring into her back as she rode away. Keeley had ridden away from Prue two or three times before and, glancing back, each time found Prue's gaze on her. Keeley wasn't going to turn around this time. Prue had said she was too rough on Jingles, and right now, knowing that Prue was righter than the rain still pouring down, Keeley just did not want to witness her accusing look.

Chapter Two

Keeley arrived home just before dark, riding Jingles sparingly, properly cooling him down, making sure she never touched his sides with her spurs. She pulled up before the barn and dropped to the ground, then slipped the saddle and blanket off and wiped Jingles dry before throwing a second blanket across his back. She put him in a stall and fed him, then headed for the soddy. Through the door's glass window a lantern glowed, warmly welcoming her home. She opened it and went inside.

"I never heard you come in. Did you win?" Attie

Webster flew at her, unmindful of the mud and stench clinging to Keeley's clothing. "Did you?" Her dark brown eyes glowed, and her small, lithe frame fit perfectly within Keeley's strong arms.

"I'm getting you all muddy," Keeley said, tossing her hat onto a nail in the wall. "I was gonna take a bath in the creek, but it's darned cold out there." She shuddered, and her teeth clacked together. "This is one weird storm."

"Oh, I don't care about mud." Attie leaped back and danced tiny steps. "Tell me what happened." Her honey-brown hair hung loose and flowing around her shoulders; her green gingham dress smelled fresh and gracefully accented her movements. She was still tan from the previous summer's sun, having refused to wear a hat since the one she'd held so dear — the only one she'd ever worn — had finally dis- integrated to a pile of broken straw around her ears.

"I won a hundred dollars."

Attie squealed with delight and grabbed Keeley, kissing her soundly. "I knew you would, Keeley. I knew it! Here, let me help you out of these wet clothes. You must be freezing."

Keeley dug into her pocket, dumping bills and change onto the table. Attie scooped it up and counted it. "It's a little short."

"I lost some in the mud. What's there?"

"Ninety-five dollars and two bits."

"Close enough." Keeley would explain the loss later. Now all she wanted to do was collapse.

Layer by layer, Attie peeled off Keeley's clothes, tossing them in a heap near the wood-slab table until Keeley stood naked and shivering before the fire. "We need to get you warm, Keeley."

Keeley's chest ached for Attie; the way she took care of her, did little things for her all the time, never complained. She stood with her back to the flames leaping in the large fireplace and drank in the odors of quail roasting on the spit. "Smells good in here, Attie."

"Got me a quail at a hundred yards first thing this morning," Attie said cheerfully. "Used your pa's Winchester. Hope you don't mind."

Keeley smiled. "Anytime. You're a real good shot."

"Sit down and soak your feet," Attie said. "I've got a bucket of water warming up." She drew up a chair before the fire and threw a blanket around Keeley's shoulders before plunking her down. She brought the promised bucket, and Keeley tested it with a toe before dunking her feet and sighing with deep pleasure.

Attie draped Keeley's wet clothing here and there around the soddy. "How's the water? Not too hot?"

Keeley moaned with contentment before saying, "Just right, honey. Perfect."

Attie knelt at Keeley's feet and began to knead her calves. Keeley could feel her muscles loosen under Attie's firm touch. It continuously amazed Keeley that she could think so much of Attie and still have such strong sensations toward Prue the way she did. There were times when she hated herself for it. She felt mean and small and disloyal. At the moment she didn't; she wanted only to be with Attie. She began to stroke Attie's hair as Attie ran a warm, wet cloth over Keeley's mud-spattered face.

"Even with my eyes closed I can still see exactly how pretty you are, Keeley," Attie said. She drew the damp cloth along the angular bones of Keeley's jaw. "You look so strong. Stronger than a man sometimes and still so soft that you melt my heart. At times," she said in a near whisper, her eyes opened only a tiny bit, "you look like you're carved from granite. Especially when you stand in the shadow of the soddy with the sun covering half your face and the house shading the other half. You look strong as stone, then, Keeley." She set aside the rag and dried Keeley's face with a corner of the blanket.

Keeley smiled, her high cheekbones changing her normally frowning face to one of sharp beauty. Her chin came to a chiseled point. Her forehead was high, and her eyebrows slim tan things that would fade in color as the summer months lengthened. She was short and compact, with a great deal of life stored in a small space.

"I like the looks of you, Keeley Delaney," Attie said. "And I like the feel and the taste of you."

Keeley heart began to race as it did every time Attie started talking to her this way. Attie touched Keeley's hair and withdrew small clots of dried mud from the strands. "I can't even tell what color your hair is," she said humorously.

Keeley smiled. "It's supposed to look brown."

"Looks like horse dung. Smells it too."

Keeley laughed. "I'll wash it after supper. Right now I'm starving."

"Then I'll feed you, my horsewoman." Attie filled a plate with quail, canned green beans and potatoes.

"I mean I'm hungry for you, Attie." Prue was far from her thoughts now.

"I know that," Attie said, handing Keeley the

17

plate. "But I don't want you fainting dead away from hunger when we . . ." Her voice trailed off as she shyly closed her eyes.

Keeley loved that about Attie. She could be so bold one minute, rubbing Keeley's bare thighs, and the next, barely able to say a word about what was going to happen to them in a short while. She smiled and ate. Attie knelt again at her feet and ran her hands along the insides of Keeley's thighs.

Keeley managed to clean her plate, but only to please Attie. Now freed of her pampering, Keeley set aside the dish and stood. The blanket fell away. Attie rose with her.

Keeley threw back the bed's heavy quilt as Attie slipped off her shoes. As she rushed to remove Attie's dress, Keeley's cold fingers trembled. "Come on," she said. "It's chilly out here." They crawled in, threw themselves at each other and pulled the quilt over their heads. They waited for their body-heat to warm them. When it had, Keeley burrowed deeper beneath the blanket and buried her face against Attie's belly. "You are so soft, Attie. Softer than a cloud."

"You don't have a single notion of how soft a cloud is, Keeley Delaney." Attie's hands anchored themselves in Keeley's hair, still gritty but now dry.

"If they're not soft like you, my darling, then they're not soft at all." Her voice came out muffled as she scooted lower. Keeley imagined the blanket took on the look of a buffalo's humped back as she made her way between Attie's sweet thighs.

"You know what you want tonight, Keeley?"

"I know exactly what I want, Attie. I been swallowing dust and mud and rain all day, and I'm ready for some sweet cream and strawberries." She

18

buried her face against the soft, thin hair between Attie's thighs and rested, drinking in the smell of her and absorbing her warmth.

Attie released Keeley's hair, her hands coming to rest on her lover's shoulders. "I need you tonight, Keeley. I need you right there."

Keeley muttered, "Why?" and began that slow, firm licking that Attie loved so much.

"It brings you closer to me." She spoke between sharp intakes of breath. "I feel like you been away a million years."

Keeley moaned an incoherent reply and continued stroking Attie until Attie began to whimper. Keeley took Attie's nipple between her thumb and forefinger. She lightly pinched it and rolled it back and forth. Attie moaned, and Keeley pinched just a little harder, causing Attie to heave and shudder. "You're close, Attie, honey."

Attie dug her fingers into Keeley's shoulders, screaming oaths of faith and loyalty.

Keeley stopped moving. Tears sprang to her eyes. She cared for Attie so that at times she could hardly bear it. She pulled herself up alongside Attie and let her tears fall.

Attie cuddled her closely. "You're as good a woman as ever walked this earth."

"And so are you, Attie, dear."

Attie lay still as Keeley rolled on top of her. Attie kept her legs together as Keeley spread hers and positioned herself against Attie.

"You have fine bones, honey," Keeley said as she moved against Attie's hips. "You fit me just right."

"You can do what you want with me."

Keeley went a little crazy every time Attie said

that. Her hip movements increased, and heat built between her legs, crawling into her belly and reaching to the ends of her toes and fingertips. She breathed faster and louder and felt a fervor within melting her to jelly. Soon the room seemed hay-loft hot on a mid-summer's day, and she cried out joyfully, unable to control her weeping. She collapsed sobbing against Attie's shoulder.

Attie held her, stroking her back. "It was a hard race, wasn't it? Do you want to talk about it?"

And Keeley did. All except the part about Prue. It didn't seem worth bringing up.

Keeley rose naked before the sun was up while Attie slept on. It was much warmer this morning, but still a bit chilly in the soddy. She fumbled around until she found some matches and got a couple of lamps and the fireplace going. That done, she walked upstream along the bank of the creek. She sat on her favorite flat rock located in the middle of the stream and washed yesterday's mud-fight from her body, gasping as each cold handful of water splashed over her, causing her to suck in huge gulps of air until her chest ceased aching from the shock.

In the cabin, she drew on clean clothes, then shimmied into her still wet boots. Over the small woodstove, she fried four eggs and a dozen thick slices of bacon cut from a slab hanging overhead. When the meat was scorched to perfection, she put it aside on a thick, white ceramic plate, then sliced potatoes and onions into the sizzling bacon fat. She fried these to crisp wafers and scraped them onto the eggs. The whole meal was washed down with three cups of coffee. When she felt the black brew wake her, she gave Attie, who still wasn't moving, a peck on the cheek, picked up her gloves and headed for the barn.

Jingles nickered when she rolled back the door. Pa hadn't done a great job of building the barn even though he'd used elm, hickory and oak trees found over on the banks of the Missouri. That had been twelve years ago. Keeley shut her mind to the thought because when she remembered that she thought of the rest of her family: Ma and her little brother, Aaron. All three of them were dead.

As grueling as yesterday's race had been, neither Jingles nor she seemed to be in too bad shape this morning. She saddled him and rode toward the north pasture where, for the past several months, she had been breaking and training a dozen wild mustangs of mixed colors.

Originally, they weren't worth two dollars a head. They were skinny and wild, and they'd hated her, but she had worked with them daily until they were fat, sleek and obedient. They were shod, the stallions gelded, and each one worth at least twenty-five dollars . . .

Today, she intended to sell them to the Army at Fort Omaha. The troops would be getting a good bunch of well-trained animals, and she'd come away with a pile of cash. With it, she would buy a good sturdy wagon to replace her rickety one, and in the fall she'd use it to haul fresh vegetables to the fort.

With as much money as she would have by day's end plus yesterday's winnings, she shouldn't have to work for quite some time. Maybe she'd find a horse good enough to race, and train him next. It's what she really wanted to do, not this busting her rump all over the prairie breaking broncos and teaching them to stand fast when a gun went off by their heads, then helping Attie in the fields picking potato bugs and cabbageworms off the crops.

The saddle creaked as she rode beneath the rising sun. She thought about their small soddy as she looked over her spread. Inside the house was a table and two chairs, the woodstove, large fireplace and a good bed. She and Addie owned a few plates and cups, some simple flatware and not much else, unless she counted the expensive glass window she'd ordered from the Montgomery Ward & Co. catalogue. It was the only luxury she had ever bought, and on the coldest mornings when the cabin's door was closed against the brutal winds that swept across the land, she often found herself staring through it as she drank her morning coffee and watched night turn into day.

Her gaze traveled across the land her pa had once owned. The Delaney spread was located within five miles of the Missouri River and Omaha City, and that made it a good place to live. Whatever crops she and Attie grew could be shipped by boat if they chose, or delivered elsewhere by wagon.

The Delaney family had worked impossibly hard at crop farming until only Keeley was left alive. They didn't have the strength, equipment or knowledge to be successful. Ma went first from exhaustion, then Pa fell beneath the hooves of a wild horse he'd sworn he'd break. When Aaron died of a terrible cough six months later, Keeley vowed she would never work that hard at farming. Someday, somehow, she would earn so much money that she'd never have to lift another finger except to feed herself.

Now she owned Pa's six hundred and forty acres, and it was proving to be a good place to raise and train horses.

She spent the morning rounding up the herd and driving it to the fort. At midday she drew up a few yards outside the palisade walls. Two sentries stood guard on either side of the opened, double-wide doors.

"I got horses to sell," she said to the soldiers. Dust swirled as the band settled to a stop. The sun was blistering hot. Not a drop of moisture was left from yesterday's deluge.

A sentry briskly nodded and trotted inside. Returning, he was followed by a bearded soldier with plenty of stripes on his blue blouse. His hat hung low over his face. He stepped close to her side.

"You a woman?" he asked. He hadn't yet glanced at the stock.

She ignored his insolence. "Who are you?"

"Sergeant Major Frazier Chappell, Cavalry."

"Then you know a good horse when you see one, Sergeant Major. This is a real good bunch." With the back of her sleeve, she wiped away sweat rolling down her cheeks. "I got twelve good animals here shod, gelded, full broke to the saddle and the sound of gunshots. No need to train them. Just get on and ride."

He turned aside and spat. A fine stream of tobacco struck the ground with a splat. "They look like buzzard bait."

His words startled her, but she remained impassive. "They ain't."

"You train them?" He gaped at her chest. A floppy-brimmed hat shadowed his eyes, and his shirtsleeves were rolled to his elbows. Sweat stains the size of pie plates darkened the armpits. Gray suspenders held up his dark blue pants worn tucked into tight, calf-high black boots. He continued scrutinizing her.

"You wanna check out the horses or me, soldier?" she said, tugging on the wide, worn brim of her own hat.

He let loose with another stream of brown fluid. It struck Jingles' leg. The horse didn't move. "Got him pretty well trained, don't you?"

"He ain't for sale. Just the rest of the bunch. And that's how well trained they all are."

The soldier circled the horses without comment, running a hand along the flanks of some, checking the teeth of a few others. He drew a pistol and fired into the air. The entire herd started but didn't prance. They settled down immediately.

"Bunch a damn house pets," he said.

"They ain't no house pets," she protested loudly.

"Listen, lady. It is lady, ain't it? I can't use these animals."

"Yeah, it's lady, Sergeant, and why the hell not? They're the best broke horses this fort's ever gonna see."

"They're too well broke. The men won't have nothing to do. They won't have the chance to learn one damn thing on a horse that's so saddle-broke, he can't learn to get back in the saddle if he's throwed."

Keeley snatched off her hat and scratched her head. "Well, if that don't beat all. I should think you'd want your men to stay in the saddle, not fall out of it."

"A soldier has to learn to fit his mount, to train

him to fit the soldier. Can't use your horses, lady." He turned to leave.

"You're lying, pony-boy." He whirled, his eyes blazing. She repeated, "You're lying. You're not buying because they're woman-broke."

He walked up to her, stopping within six inches of her stirrup. "That's right, lady. I want man-broke horses. A horse broke by a woman ain't worth shit. It's a milksop horse. Only good for drawing a buggy on a sunny day or for some kid to play with."

"How about I show you how wrong you are? I can make any one of them rear if I want him to or turn a corner so tight he'll dig a hole. You already saw what they do when you shoot a gun near them."

"Can't use 'em," he repeated, and walked back toward the fort.

She jammed on her hat and yelled, "Getup, ponies!"

The sergeant major stumbled out of the way as Keeley circled the bunch and drove them inside the walls. "Close the damn doors," he yelled to the guards, but it was already too late.

Once inside, the horses bunched up. Trained to ground-tie, they wouldn't go anywhere. She dismounted, stripped Jingles' tack from him and threw it on the nearest horse. She mounted up and rode easily, turning left then right while the sergeant watched. She commanded the mustang to pivot first one way, then the other. For her closing act, she ran him the length of the fort and back before coming to a screeching halt where she had first started. Soldiers gathered to watch, cheering and encouraging her. Only the sergeant major stood grim-faced.

She dismounted and whipped off the tack,

throwing it onto another mount and repeating her performance twice more. Then, breathing hard, she saddled Jingles and rode over to the sergeant and waited.

He rolled his chaw from one cheek to the other, then spat. "You got nothing but circus horses. The Army ain't no circus."

The men watching had fallen silent, listening to the exchange. A young soldier of not more than eighteen approached her. "I'd sure like a horse like that, miss. The one I got busts my tail every time I git on him. What'll you take for one?"

"Thirty doll —"

Sergeant Major Chappell whirled. "She ain't selling these nags, Private. Get back to your duty."

"Hey, he can buy a horse if he wants," Keeley shouted.

"The hell he can. He'll ride Army-trained, and that's all he'll ride. Now, get the hell out of this fort and take these pregnant cows with you. Come in here riling my men. Damn women, anyway. Get on outta here, now!"

Dust floated thick in the air as Keeley sat rigidly in the saddle. She wished she was sitting up to her neck in creek water, cooling the flush of embarrassment and anger consuming her as he yelled and cursed at her in front of the troops. Holding her head arrogantly high, she drove her horses out of the fort.

Chapter Three

Dejectedly, she rode toward town, driving her band before her. She fought hard to avoid hating her sex. Men always had it better. *Always*. Now what she going to do with all these horses?

Leaving the herd at the outskirts, she rode into Omaha and tied up before Prue's restaurant, thinking she would console herself with a cup of boiling hot coffee to add to the already scorching heat. Today's weather was as unusually hot as yesterday's had been cold. She was glad of it. The more miserable she could make herself feel, the better she'd enjoy it. She could also look at Prue's sky-blue eyes, which was what drew her here in the first place.

Overhead, a small doorbell tinkled announcing her as she walked in. The tap of her boot-steps and jingling spurs echoed loudly in the long room.

At this hour, the place was empty except for a couple of die-hard regulars seated at the counter. Later, the diner would fill with cowhands, farmers, businessmen and soldiers looking for a quick bite, or an all-out delicious home-cooked meal, before heading home.

Prue wasn't around, but Keeley slumped herself down at the counter anyway. Prue's young redheaded cook and waiter, Timmy Block, poured her a coffee. He gave her his familiar big-toothed, broad smile. Timmy was tall and his joints seemed held together with loose thongs with a few muscles and skin thrown over it all, making him look like a long, lean hank of rope.

"Where's Prue?" she asked. She took a sip and flinched at the heat, watching Timmy empty an ashtray and wipe it clean using the same cloth with which he'd just finished wiping the counter. Prue would skin him if she caught him.

"At the church."

"As usual."

Through his pale freckled face, Timmy grinned again.

Keeley finished up and tossed a half-dime on the counter. Maybe she'd take time to stop and say hi to Prue, who was always doing something for somebody — collecting clothes for poor folks, delivering medicine when Doc was too busy to, baking extra cookies for the children around town. She wasn't overbearing about her acts of charity, or even deliberate. Prue Morris was just plain kind and went out of her way for others. These days her big dream was to see a belfry built on the church, which doubled as the town's school, and a big brass bell installed.

Keeley thought her friend a little foolish, doing the extra work she did for people she didn't even know that well and sometimes not at all. But over time, Prue's popularity had grown around Omaha. She was terribly pretty; even so, she was trusted by the wives of men who frequented her restaurant. There'd never been a scandal or reason to believe there might be. Prue Morris remained a perfect lady.

Unlike Prue, Keeley thought entirely differently about aiding others. She wouldn't have given a thirsty man water. Uppity damn town, Omaha. She hated the place and couldn't wait to build her fortune and get out. She didn't care where she landed as long as it was far from here. Nobody'd helped the Delaneys when they'd most needed it, and nobody had come to any of the funerals that Keeley had conducted alone, never mind digging the graves where she'd planated the single tree after Aaron died. The tree, an oak standing about six feet high now, was the one piece of greenery she didn't mind taking care of. She watered it frequently, ensuring that her family would always have shade to give them respite from the summer's hot sun.

As she walked to the church, Jingles complacently followed her, bumping her back with his nose. She threw his reins over the hitching rail then walked inside, respectfully removing her hat.

Prue sat in a front pew looking at something in her lap. Hearing Keeley, she turned and smiled, making Keeley feel warm and special. "You don't have to remove your hat in here, Keeley. Only the men do."

Keeley flushed and donned it again, tipping it back so that her face wasn't half-covered by the drooping brim. "That better?"

"Much." Prue gestured with a hand. "Come, take a look at what I've got." Her fine Eastern accent caressed Keeley's ears as she joined Prue. Beside her were strewn several rough drawings.

"I've made a few sketches of what I'd like to see for a church bell," Prue said happily. "What do you think?" She held a sheet at arm's length. "This one is my favorite."

"Didn't know the place needed a bell," Keeley said practically. "People seem to get here on time for school and for church every Sunday."

Prue chuckled and touched Keeley's sleeve. "They do, Keeley. But wouldn't it be wonderful to hear a bell greeting the children on school days and ringing joyfully on Sunday mornings, welcoming everybody, and then afterward, celebrating the Lord as they left?"

Keeley shrugged. "Couldn't really say." She'd never gone to church. She wasn't uncomfortable inside this one, but to her, it was just another building, like the emporium or the gun shop, holding no particular significance. Prue's hand came to rest on her arm. Now *that* held significance. Her light touch made Keeley's skin burn right through her sleeve.

"Well, Miss Keeley, I think a bell would sound beautiful tolling over the plains for all to hear, calling people to worship. Maybe one day we could have more than one. But," she said, sighing, "just one would be incredibly expensive."

"How much?"

"It depends upon the size," Prue explained, leaning against Keeley's shoulder. Keeley wondered if Prue was deliberately plaguing her by sitting so close, so friendly. She'd always behaved that way toward Keeley, and it rattled her thinking. She never could decide if she liked her head rattling like that or not. Prue was saying, "The better the tone, the more the bell will cost. Size is involved, and how much time it takes to cast it and test its tone and strength. You wouldn't want the thing to crack at the first good yank of the rope. Many things are considered."

"You know a lot about bells." Keeley knew nothing.

"The Pass and Stowe Bell Foundry is in Philadelphia, Pennsylvania, where I was born and raised. My father worked there until he died. He used to talk about bells all the time. Mother and I got pretty sick of hearing about them, but now I'm glad I listened. I consider myself an expert bellwoman, although I've never been near the foundry."

Keeley remained silent as Prue continued discussing the metals used in making bells.

Out of politeness Keeley asked, "Ain't bronze, bronze?"

"No." Prue's eyes shone as she spoke knowledgeably and enthusiastically. "A good cast bell is made of bell metal, four parts copper and one part tin. Anything less," she said, gathering the remaining sketches and leafing through them, "doesn't give as good a tone. You want something rich sounding. Especially here where the land is so flat. People would be able to hear the bell peal for miles around."

Keeley thought maybe people wouldn't want to

hear the thing clanging clear out onto the prairie. Aloud, she said, "But you could get a cheaper bell, if you wanted to, that still rang good, right?"

Prue smiled. "It's possible. But I'm a bit fussy, you see. I want the best bell there is."

"Why? Why not just the next-best bell or the one under that?"

"Because this is Omaha, and this is my home for the rest of my life, and because I want quality whenever possible. I think this is very possible if enough people are willing to help work for it."

"Sounds like a waste of money if you can get a bell for less and ring it, and it does the same job that a real expensive bell does."

"I suppose, but why not have the best if it's possible, Keeley?" Prue asked. Keeley heard just a hint of irritation in her voice. "Don't you want it for yourself?"

Keeley gave that a moment's thought. "I do," she said. "And I aim to have it too."

Prue leaned against the pew, crossing her arms in front of her and cradling her large breasts. "And what might that be, Miss Keeley? You already have a good piece of land that produces excellent vegetables and canned goods. Everyone says so."

Attie didn't do laundry anymore. She raised and sold the vegetables. During fall, she canned for days, selling most of them. The money she earned kept her and Keeley afloat until the following growing season. She loved gardening, while Keeley thought the whole enterprise a backbreaking job. "It's better than doing laundry," Attie had crisply retorted one day.

Unable to maintain Prue's steady look, Keeley focused her attention on the church: a plain oak podium to the left; a small pedal organ and bench and fifteen straight-backed chairs for the choir to the right; a heavier, more ornate oak chair nearby for the minister when his duties didn't demand that he stand; a plain cross attached to the wall behind the altar. "I'd like to make a lot of money and get out of Omaha."

"Why?" Prue asked, surprised.

"I don't want to die working." Never before had Keeley uttered a word to anyone regarding her feelings, including Attie. "My whole family did, and I don't want to, too."

"You won't, Keeley." Again Prue put her hand on Keeley's arm. "That was your family, not you. You work harder than anyone I know. Breaking horses, racing, farming. Why, you're as fit as a fiddle."

Keeley's eyes became large, filling with fear. "Doesn't mean it can't happen. I don't want to live like that — or die like that. I want to take it easy in my lifetime."

Prue withdrew her hand, folding both in her lap. "Then it's a good idea that you took that girl into your soddy. I'm sure she's a big help."

"She is," Keeley said. Bitterly, she added, "But once I make my fortune, I'll never pick up a hoe again. Never!"

"Keeley." Prue paused. Keeley looked her way. "There is always education. You could become a teacher, a doctor —"

"A doctor? Or a teacher? I'm not the type to want to do either one of them things. I got to be outside moving all the time. You know, doing things. I got to move!"

Prue sighed. She remained pensive for a while before asking, "How is your fortune coming along?

33

You'll need a considerable amount to live on to do nothing for the rest of your life."

"I'm getting there," Keeley briefly answered.

"And then what will you do with all that free time? You don't like to sit around. You just said so."

"I been thinking about getting me a good racehorse. I'm a good rider. I could do that."

"That's work. There's training, practice, getting up early. And you can't just race mustangs. They're not real racehorses. You need quarter horses or thoroughbreds."

"I don't know about those kinds of horses. But even so, training racehorses ain't work."

"Really?" Prue's eyebrows rose.

"I like doing hard work . . ." Keeley'd walked into that one. Damn this Prue woman! She left Keeley feeling befuddled every time she was in the same room with her. Keeley rose abruptly. "I can't be wasting my time sitting around here gabbing all day. I got horses to sell." She gave her pants a tug. "Fort Omaha don't need this bunch."

Prue remained seated, her hands still primly folded in her lap. "I assume your horses weren't ready enough for the Army. The soldiers are pretty fussy sometimes."

"Sometimes," Keeley answered, sidestepping the real truth. "I'll try Fort Niobrara. It's quiet on the plains these days. I should be all right. I'll leave in the morning. Might's well get an early start."

Prue walked her to the door. "That's a long way. A couple hundred miles from here, isn't it?"

"A little more." Keeley didn't want to ride to Niobrara. It *was* a long way. She didn't want to put the miles on her animals, and she didn't want to be away from Omaha that long because she would miss Attie. And Prue.

At the door, Prue said, "Good luck, Keeley. Let me know how things turn out. I'm sure you'll do well."

Keeley nodded and touched her hat with a gloved finger. She mounted up and headed for the emporium. She'd need extra supplies to go so far. Probably cost her half her winnings. She was never going to get ahead if selling horses was going to be like this. By the time she got home and turned the band out to pasture that evening, she was as cranky as a wet cat.

Attie insisted on fussing over her like she was an old woman when she would just as soon have been left alone for a while. To further test her patience, Prue drove up just as Attie was starting supper. "Thought I'd take a chance that you two hadn't eaten yet." Her smile was lovely and warming.

Standing in the doorway in her stocking feet, Keeley squelched her surprise. Attie, also shoeless, stood close by Keeley's side in her linsey-woolsey dress. Prue still wore the lovely pale blue taffeta dress she'd had on earlier today.

"Are you two hungry?" Prue asked cordially.

"Always," Keeley replied, smiling, answering for both her and Attie.

"Is she right about you, Miss Attie?" Prue asked. "Are you hungry too?"

Attie blushed a brilliant red. "I can rustle up something real quick, Miss Morris." She turned away to begin cooking, but Prue called her back.

"Oh, goodness, call me Prue, Attie. And do stay. No need for you to cook anything this evening. This is my treat."

Prue stepped from the single-seated carriage and

grasped a picnic basket while Keeley released the horse from the harness. "Just take a minute or two to hitch him back up," she said. "I'll just put him in the corral next to the barn."

Prue and Attie waited at the door. "Thank you, Keeley," Prue said. She had never been here before. Keeley wondered why she was here at all and what she thought of the place. Inside, Prue set the basket on the table, then ran a hand along its plank surface. "Very nice, Keeley. What kind of wood is it?"

"Oak. Pa made it for Ma right after we moved here."

"Beautiful work." It was a rough table. Keeley knew it. Prue was just flattering her.

Prue wandered around the small interior while Attie watched with catlike eyes, and Keeley watched Attie. She wondered what Attie was thinking, hoping Attie couldn't hear her thundering heart. She felt dishonest, having Prue in her home with Attie there too.

"Curtains on the window. Glass. You live well." Prue fingered the plain, white linen curtains. She turned toward Attie. "Did you make the curtains?" Attie nodded. "Very nice sewing." She studied the tiny, precise stitches Attie had used to hem the cloth.

"I like a lot of light," Keeley said. "Makes me feel better somehow."

"Helping people makes me feel like that," Prue answered. "But fine things do too."

"Like bells that cost a lot."

"For one. China dishes?" She had picked up a dish from a stack on the shelf over the sink.

"My ma's," Attie answered. "We never use them."

Again, Keeley wondered exactly why Prue had come.

"Of course."

"We use ceramic," Attie said.

Keeley waited for Prue to laugh. She didn't.

"That's wise and prudent. I use ceramic in my restaurant. Upstairs in my apartment, I use china. It's a set that was given to me by a friend from a long time ago."

Keeley experienced a twinge of jealousy. She let it die. "Not likely you'd have ceramic," she replied, still standing aside while Prue continued surveying the small interior.

"No, I admit that I vainly eat from my china each evening."

"Nice to be rich," Keeley commented shyly.

"No, just fortunate to have had a mother who sent along a few nice things with me when I moved out here a couple of years ago. And of course, the friend who gave me the china. Here, I've talked and gawked long enough. Let me show you what I've brought along." She lifted a red and white checkered cloth from the basket and removed chicken, rolls and baked potatoes all kept warm with small heated soapstones wrapped in thick cotton cloth and placed in the bottom of the basket. There were also three pieces of cherry pie. "You looked pretty tired this afternoon at the church," she said smiling and looking directly at Keeley.

Keeley glanced at Attie. She hadn't told Attie she'd stopped there. She had said instead, that she'd come straight home from the emporium. Attie's eyes bore into Keeley's as Keeley smiled her broadest smile and enthusiastically patted Attie's shoulder. "Well, I wasn't, so there was no need to go to so much fuss, Prue. But we're glad you did, ain't we, Attie? Now you won't have to go cooking tonight. You can have a vacation for once."

Attie brought over three plates from the cupboard. "I'm grateful, Prue." She smiled, but Keeley could see it was forced. "It's true enough, there's not much time to sit around this place. None at all, in fact. Sometimes, though" — she brushed aside a strand of loose hair that had escaped her ponytail — "I'd just love to sit back, put my feet up on the table and have me a cup of coffee like the men do down at your restaurant." A plate banged heavily against the tabletop.

"I don't allow the men to put their feet anywhere except on the floor." Prue chuckled. "And they can't spit, either."

"Well, that's a fine place you have, Prue," Keeley said, setting out cups and generally trying to be helpful. "Hey, Attie, how'd you like you and me to go there and have a cup of coffee sometime and maybe a sweet bun too?"

"Are there sweet buns there?" Another plate banged down.

"A couple of kinds," Prue said. "And pie. Seems like I can't keep enough pie in the place."

"I'll bet Keeley loves your pie," Attie said in carefully clipped words. The final plate landed.

"Yes, she does," Prue replied while serving the chicken. "Especially apple."

"Dried apple, right?" Attie took a seat at the table.

"Hm, maybe she likes cherry the best."

Keeley joined them. "Don't like either the best," she grumbled. "I'm partial to pumpkin, so you're both wrong." She picked up the bowl of potatoes and carefully placed the largest on Attie's plate and the smallest on her own before passing the remaining one to Prue.

"Well, then," Prue said, helping herself. "We'll have to see about getting some pumpkin pies made, won't we, Attie?"

"Lot of work, making a punkin' pie."

"Then I'll make one and bring it to you both. How's that?"

"Why, that'd be just fine, wouldn't it, Attie?" Keeley was grinning, hoping that Attie would be equally pleased.

"If you're inclined." Attie bit into her chicken. Crisp golden flakes of coating dropped to her plate.

Prue took tiny bites, eating daintily, making Keeley keenly aware of Attie's crude manners as well as her own. Since Ma had died, Keeley didn't care how her food got into her mouth. She set down the chicken leg and cut off a piece with her knife. It wasn't as small a bite as Prue's, but it wasn't a whole darned chicken half, either. She wiped her mouth carefully with her sleeve.

The rest of the meal passed in silence. Keeley felt as though the air were tinder, and the tiniest spark would start the whole place blazing. She could tell that Attie was plenty mad at her for lying. Why hadn't she told Attie she'd stopped at the church? Attie wouldn't have cared. But Keeley had deliberately gone there to see Prue, and that's what made the difference. She was sweet on Prue, and she didn't want Attie to know.

After supper, Keeley retrieved Prue's horse while Attie helped her pack up. Keeley had just finished harnessing when Attie and Prue came outside. "Thank you, Keeley." Prue took the reins from Keeley, caressing her hand as she reached for them. Was it an accident? Keeley didn't think so, but Prue was already watching where she was stepping as Attie herself gave Prue a hand into the buggy. "Thank you, too, Attie." She smiled, and Attie smiled back. Keeley wondered what they'd been talking about. They suddenly seemed pretty friendly.

"Thanks for the good food, Prue. I can see why Keeley would want to stop at your place. You're a real fine cook. Better than me."

"I doubt it. I know basics, and that's what men want. You make pies especially for Keeley. That's the best way to cook. She's lucky to have hired you."

"Why, I ain't a hired —"

Keeley took Attie's arm. "She's the best there is around, Prue. I'm lucky I found her before you did. Now you quit flattering her, or I'm gonna have to lock her up."

Attie freed her arm and pinched Keeley sharply in the back. Keeley stifled a grunt of pain, turning it into a guffaw.

Prue carefully settled her skirt around her feet. The taffeta softly rustled as it moved. "Well, I'd better be getting back. Timmy will wonder where I am. By the way, Keeley," she said in a very matter-of-fact way, "I have another idea I'd like to add to the bell's design. Next time you're in town, stop in and I'll tell you about it. I'd like to know what you think."

Keeley felt another painful pinch as she asked, "Why me? I don't know about bells and such."

"That's exactly why, Keeley. You're unspoiled. You'd be the perfect one to help me decide. Everyone else would insist that they had the only correct idea. You don't care one way or the other." She smiled and waved good-bye, her picnic basket parked securely beside her.

Keeley whirled on Attie. "You pinch me one more time, Attie, and I'm going to slap you a good one."

Attie turned on her heel and marched into the soddy.

That night they slept side by side without touching each other.

Chapter Four

Keeley awoke with a throbbing headache. Her dreams had been vicious and real. Attie had hit her over the noggin with a hoe handle while Prue stood by watching and laughing and ringing a big, black handbell that made Keeley's ears ache and her skull feel like it was splitting in two.

She groaned as she sat up. As her feet touched the floor she knew she had to get to the backhouse in the next thirty seconds or there'd be an awful mess around here. She made it in the required time and staggered back to the soddy. She was dizzy; tiny black spots floated before her eyes. She couldn't recall being sick like this in a long time, maybe never, and it scared her.

She dressed, skipping breakfast. At the creek, she splashed water on her head until her hair was drenched. It hung in her face, hiding the sweat that refused to give way to the cold water. In the soddy again, she forced down a cup of coffee. She deliberately created a racket, trying to wake Attie. Either Attie was still sleeping or still very angry.

Bundled up against a chill in spite of the heat given off by the roaring fire in the grate and her own burning fever, Keeley looked once more at where Attie lay unmoving. A cold stone lay in her chest where she normally felt a glow representing summertime all year around.

"Attie?" There was a slight shuffling of Attie's feet. "I got to be going now. I should be back in about three weeks, give or take. Do you need anything before I go?" Attie mumbled into the covers. Keeley's heart sank. She should never have lied to Attie. Never. She walked over and pulled back enough blanket so that she could kiss Attie on the cheek. "Well, like I said, I'll be back in three weeks."

"Be careful," Attie said. "I'll take care of things here."

Shame engulfed Keeley. "I know. You'll do a fine job too."

Attie didn't respond. After standing there a full two minutes, Keeley left and headed for the barn.

It took her longer than usual to get herself together and round up the horses. Those animals were supposed to have been gone yesterday, and she was supposed to be sleeping late this morning.

She added Jingles to the herd and rode another. Two hundred and twenty-five miles. She wondered if she could make ten today. Maybe if she camped early for the next couple of days, she'd be okay. She sure didn't want to die out there.

Motivated by such thoughts, Keeley didn't stop after having traveled only ten miles, but pushed on for twenty before making camp beside a good running stream with plenty of grass for the horses. Unless there was a major storm brewing or thieves lurking about, the horses wouldn't wander too far during the night.

She ate hardtack and drank from the stream before rolling into her blankets for the night.

The sun rose hot over the near-flat plains. Not a single tree grew and only a very few bushes. If a body wanted to be alone, the middle of Nebraska was the place to come.

Keeley had slept well beyond her usual time and woke drenched in sweat with the same relentlessly pounding headache that had plagued her the day before. She cast aside her blanket and cursed herself upright. She relieved herself several yards from camp, then doused her face and neck at the creek. The water cooled her, and the headache abated slightly, giving her hope that she was on the mend.

Thirty minutes later, she mounted her own horse and gathered the herd. "I might make it yet, Jingles." She often spoke to him when riding alone. He helped her think things through.

An angry cloud of doom descended upon her as she envisioned a hundred reasons Fort Niobrara wouldn't buy her horses. After building up a good head of steam over it, her thoughts darkened further. She recalled Attie's reaction to Prue's unannounced visit and her fancy food, then letting on that Keeley had visited Prue that day when Keeley had clearly avoided saying anything to Attie.

Again she asked herself why she hadn't said something about having seen Prue. It was the same as lying when she'd skipped that part and did so every time she thought about Prue or saw her. They weren't fair notions to have, not with how she and Attie carried on in that soddy.

Several horses began to drift away from the rest of the herd, and she yelled at them, "Come on, you crow baits. You're turning into real pains in the behind." She spurred her mount, then got them bunched and moving forward again. "What am I getting mad for?" she asked aloud. "It does nothing but make me feel more miserable than I already do." She took a bead on the horizon and dozed in the saddle, checking from time to time to see that she was still headed in the right direction and that the herd was too.

It took her two weeks to reach the fort. She was saddle-weary and still a mite on the sick side. She had finally concluded that Prue's chicken hadn't been cooked enough and that's why she'd gotten sick. Keeley hoped that Attie was okay. She didn't think she could get along without Attie. Attie had become a big part of her life over the past two years.

She approached the palisade and shouted, "Hello, the gates!" From the top of the wall, seven rifle barrels pointed at her. She ignored them and announced, "I got horses to sell. Who wants to look them over?"

The gates opened, and a blond, bareheaded lieutenant walked out of the fort. Keeley kept her hat pulled low and spoke in a gruff voice. "Gun-broke, saddle-broke and trained to ground-tie. Healthy and well-behaved. Thirty dollars a head."

The lieutenant, who didn't look more than twenty years old, inspected the herd. He stepped back and fired his pistol. Flinching and jerking their heads, the horses stayed where they were. "Saddle one of them," he said.

"I'm on one now, Lieutenant," she answered. "Here's what else they can do." She took the mustang through its paces then pulled up before the officer.

"Give you twenty-five a head."

"Thirty," Keeley pushed. She had hoped to get twenty if she got anything. Not expecting to sell at all, she went for a big price. Her heart raced, her head already calculating the amount.

"Twenty-eight, and that's it," the lieutenant said.

"Done."

Keeley slipped from the saddle and removed her tack. "Jingles there is mine. This one is yours."

"Good enough," the lieutenant said. "See the pay-master."

"Cash only," Keeley said outright. She wouldn't take a check. How was she to know there was money in the bank to cover it when she went to cash it two weeks from now?

The young lieutenant agreed. "Private," he said to one of the sentries, "stable these horses, and show this man where the paymaster's office is."

The sentry saluted. "Yes, sir." Before taking charge of the herd, he pointed Keeley in the right direction. "Right over there, mister. Second cabin." In both instances, Keeley wisely let her true identity pass. She didn't have the money in her pocket yet.

The fort contained several low buildings constructed of sod. The place looked worn and tired.
Outside the soddies, men sat around looking bored as
they chewed tobacco and blades of grass. Keeley
guessed there was little to do here. Maybe the horses
would liven them up if some of the soldiers didn't
have mounts, which was sometimes the case.

She was paid three hundred thirty-six dollars in
gold coin. The small leather sack rested heavy in her
hand. She tucked it into her pocket along with a bill
of sale for twelve horses received in good order. "You
need a place to stay tonight?" the barrel-chested, mus-
tachioed paymaster asked.

"Thanks, but I'll be moving on." She pulled her
hat even lower over her face.

The paymaster nodded and returned to his books.
Keeley left the fort feeling halfway well in body and
joyous in heart.

Alternating easy lopes and walks, she rode twenty
miles before making camp. She took great comfort in
her blanket that evening with her head resting on the
saddle. The money pouch gouged her hip, so she
removed it and shoved it into a nearby saddlebag
before resettling herself. She gazed at the blazing stars
above, watched dozens of them fall through the night
blackness, then peacefully drifted into sleep.

The following morning she was as sick as ever,
sweating and coughing. It was a test to see if she
would even be able to stand after squatting to relieve
herself. She did by first rolling to her side, then
pushing herself upward, using her arms that she was
sure would give way beneath her weight. The sun was
high before she was ready to leave. As she had on her
way to Niobrara, she took a fix on some distant land-

mark and headed for it, dozing and glancing, dozing and glancing until she reached that point, then repeated the act, eventually making twenty miles before finding a stream and collapsing to the ground for the night. She dragged herself around getting things done. How glad she was that she had sold her string. Alone, Jingles could almost take care of himself, never leaving her side during the night, grazing right around her and resting nearby.

She awoke refreshed but tired, and after a cold breakfast and an even colder creek bath, she dressed and headed out. The day went well until that evening, when she had to stop early and eat and sleep and do nothing else but lie as if she were dead.

Her lingering illness and exhaustion eventually faded until, by the time she returned home a week and a half later, she was once again herself. Hooting and hollering, she ran Jingles for the last quarter-mile to the house. She could hardly wait to show Attie her gold.

"Attie, Attie," she screamed. "I sold the horses. Every last one of them." She flew from the saddle as Jingles skidded to a stop, throwing up dirt around his feet. Attie came rushing in from the garden where she had been checking cabbage for infestation.

Keeley expected a cold reception, but Attie was laughing and shouting, "I'm so happy to see you. I've missed you. Oh, I've missed you."

Keeley grabbed her and swung her around in circles. "We're rich, Attie, rich! Our idea worked."

"Show me," Attie said. Her face was lighted up like a young summer's day.

Grinning hard, Keeley slipped her hand into the

saddlebag where, days ago, she had stuffed the money pouch. "Hold out your hands," she said, untying the thong that sealed it. "We don't want to drop a single coin." She tipped the cash into Attie's hands. They both stared, then stared again. "What the hell?" Keeley felt the blood drain from her face. She picked up a coin. "This ain't a gold piece." Disbelief, rage and frustration gripped her as she turned it over. "This ain't nothing but a common stone. So are these others. They're all stones." She slapped aside Attie's hands. The stones flew, and Attie let out a cry.

"How much was there, Keeley?" she asked timidly as she rubbed her hand.

"Three hundred and thirty-six dollars. *Three hundred and thirty-six goddamn dollars.*" Keeley collapsed to her knees. Sweat ran down her temples and along her cheeks and forehead. She looked pleadingly at Attie. "I watched the paymaster count the gold and put it in the pouch. I put it in my bag myself. How in hell did I lose it, Attie?" Savagely, she beat her fists against the ground.

Attie jumped, saying nothing. Keeley wanted to scream at her, blame her for Keeley's having to go when she was so sick, blame her for not having sold the horses right here at their own fort instead of one so far away. Unable to, she gathered the stones, one by one, and returned them to the bag. This mess wasn't Attie's fault.

"What will you do, Keeley?" Attie's voice trembled.

Keeley's body shook with wrath. "I'm going to put Jingles in the pasture, and then I'm gonna sit in the creek naked, and then I'm gonna sit in the sun, and when I'm done, I'm gonna know what happened, and then I'm gonna know what to do, and then I'm gonna do it." Her voice was a monotone, a declaration of purpose, a solemn compact with herself.

Attie backed away from her. "I'll get you some clean clothes. You'll be wanting clean clothes when you're done washing. I'll bring you some good food while you sit in the water. I'll bet you ain't had a decent meal since you left here."

"I got real sick too." Her voice became flat as she continued absorbing the terrible loss.

Attie nodded. "You look pretty thin. I'll bring hot chicken broth. It'll be good, if you've been sick."

Keeley looked up at her from her kneeling position in the dirt. "Did you get sick, Attie?"

"No."

"Wished I'd took some tea with me," Keeley said. On her feet again, she drew Attie to her, held her gently and stroked her hair. "I'm sorry, Attie. I just don't know what happened. That money was half yours. You put in your time too."

With loving hands, Attie pushed her away. "Go sit in the creek, Keeley. I'll bring you hot food. You need to rest and to think. I'll take care of Jingles too."

At the brook, Attie brought Keeley a big mug of steaming broth. Sitting naked and shivering on her rock as the water poured around her, Keeley took the cup with a quick thanks and a small but reassuring smile. Attie looked scared, and Keeley sure didn't want that, not after having left a month ago and Attie mad at her then. "I believe you might just be the best woman in all of Nebraska state."

"Thank you, my dear, sweet, strong woman."

Keeley rested her elbows on her propped-up knees and sipped the chicken stock. Her vision blurred as she fought to relive every move she'd made since leaving Fort Niobrara. Someone, somehow, had robbed her blind without her ever knowing.

Chapter Five

This time when Keeley went to town, she made sure she invited Attie. They used Attie's wagon and horse, picking up salt, sugar and coffee at the emporium. Keeley also bought a pound of nails. The barn needed some work on the west side; now would be a good time to do it.

The day was sharp and clear; warm winds blew softly; wild herds of elk and horses could be seen roaming in the distance. Attie wore a comfortable gray dress, full at the waist, while Keeley wore her usual wide-brimmed hat, blue cotton shirt and heavy pants and boots.

After leaving the emporium, they drove over to Prue's. "I'll get you a cup of coffee that you don't have to fix yourself," Keeley said. "It ain't as good as yours, but maybe it'll taste it since you don't have to make it."

Attie laughed, taking Keeley's hand as she jumped from the seat.

Omaha bustled with Saturday morning activity. People milled about or stopped to chat with one another; saloons' batwing doors busily swung back and forth; painted ladies called out from overhead porches to the men below, making some laugh and others frown.

Prue's place was also buzzing. The counter and all but one table at the rear of the room were filled. Keeley and Attie made for it before it too was taken.

"Hello, ladies." Prue came to wait on them, her hands propped lightly on her hips. She wore a tight-fitting yellow dress, leaving Keeley slightly breathless. She felt her face flush and hoped Attie wouldn't notice.

Attie didn't. She was busy herself, looking Prue over. "My, that is a beautiful dress, Prue," she said. "I've never seen such a pretty one. Looks like the sun, don't it, Keeley?"

Keeley nodded. "Sure does. But so does your blue dress. But more like the sky." Keeley knew better than to flatter just Prue.

"Coffee?" Prue asked.

"Two, please," Attie answered. "Sugar and cream for me, black for Keeley."

"I know how Keeley likes hers," Prue answered offhandedly. "And I'll fix yours up just fine too, Attie."

As she walked away, Attie glared at Keeley.

"I been here before, Attie," Keeley answered tiredly. "Now drop it right there."

"I think —"

"Drop it! Why don't you just look at the way the place has been repainted and the pictures on the walls and such?"

Light green walls held pictures of green farms from the Northeast, mountains of the West, Southern ladies in magnificent gowns riding in expensive carriages. "A little something for everyone's taste," Prue had explained to Keeley. A large calendar was tacked to the back wall and a fine pendulum clock sat on a shelf near the front wall. A big glass window in front and the paned-glass door allowed for plenty of natural light to shine through.

"It's a pretty place," Attie agreed. "Nice oak floors, clean ceiling. No grease spots. I heard people used to get sick eating here, though."

"Maybe they still do," Keeley answered. "All I ever had was pie, cookies and coffee."

Attie seemed to give Keeley's comment thought. She asked, "How bad sick did you say you got that time?"

"Headache, sick to my stomach, weak, dizzy, spots in front of my eyes."

"You think it was the chicken that Prue brought us?"

"I thought about that."

Prue appeared with the coffee. She had a sheet of paper tucked beneath one arm. "Brought you some apple pie. On the house."

"Oh, we couldn't do that," Attie said.

"Never mind. I need to talk to Keeley anyway. You enjoy your pie while I make myself at home here. Do you mind, Keeley?" Keeley sipped her coffee as Prue pulled a chair close beside her. "It's about the bell design. The town council approved the whole idea just last week. Now all we have to do is make our dream come true."

"Uh huh." Attie couldn't complain about that, Keeley thought. She'd known that Prue wanted to talk to Keeley regarding the bell.

"Tell me what you think." She laid the paper on the table. On it was the outline of a bell that encompassed most of the eight-by-ten sheet. Halfway down the bell was written: *OMAHA, March 1, 1867, Statehood*. Beneath that, the present year, 1880. Above and below the bold inscription were the names of those presently living and working in and around Omaha, including its city officials. Prue tipped the sketch toward Attie, who smiled, apparently pleased at being included in the conversation. "On the back at the top and bottom," Prue said as she flipped the sheet to show another bell with more words inscribed, "are the names of the Omaha Indians."

"You didn't leave out anybody," Attie said. She and Keeley both stared at the plan.

"What do you think, Keeley? You too, Attie. What do you two think?"

"I can't imagine that somebody can make a bell like that, Prue," Attie replied honestly. "All those tiny letters. I can't read, but it looks like a lot of work to me."

"Keeley?"

Keeley thoughtfully put a thumb to her lips, then

rubbed her chin. She continued staring at the sheet, then turned it over.

"It would be the most beautiful thing this town has ever seen," Prue said, her eyes gleaming. "Shining bronze, a rich ring calling people to church or to school."

"Or to a fire," Keeley said practically.

"Or to a fire," Prue echoed. "What a good idea!"

"Are you going to draw the final design?" Attie asked. Her coffee sat before her, cooling and forgotten.

"I don't know," Prue answered. "I thought I might make a contest out of it."

"Is there somebody around here who can draw that good?" Keeley asked.

"Have you looked at Hawk Blackbean's gun handles?" Prue said. "Or the handle on that knife of his? They're all made of ivory. He showed them to me one day when he took me for a drive. He's done some very fine carving on them. A bear on one, an eagle on —"

"You been out riding with Hawk Blackbean?" Keeley snapped.

"Yes, I have. Why?"

"Nothing," Keeley answered cautiously. "Just surprised, that's all. He's not a good man. Him and me had a fight."

Prue smiled at her. "Oh, I know. I watched from the window that day. All in good fun on Hawk's part, you being the wild woman you are. Not very good manners from either of you, but you both had a good laugh out of it. He told me." She laughed lightly. "You just don't know him. He's nothing but a big bear."

"A loco one," Attie piped in. Daintily, she sipped her coffee. Keeley smiled, pleased with Attie's remark. There was nothing like loyalty.

"Well, I'm not going to get into a discussion with either of you about Hawk Blackbean. I just want to know what you think of this design."

Keeley shrugged. Now that Blackbean might be involved, she didn't care. "Whatever suits you, Prue. You probably got good judgment here."

Attie coughed and scooped up a bite of pie.

"Hey, Prue, got any coffee left?" Tam Showalker sat at the counter. His bulk and grizzled look demanded immediate attention. Timmy had been scurrying around the room as well as behind the counter trying to keep up with orders and continuously glancing Prue's way.

"Coming, Tam," she called. "I shouldn't leave Timmy in the lurch like this," she said, picking up the design. "He looks like he's ready to shoot me. I'm glad you like the design, Keeley. I'll see how the church feels about it this Sunday. Why don't you join us?"

"Busy," Keeley said.

"Attie?"

"Same."

"Someday, you two must come. Reverend Barnes is quite good. I think you'd like him."

The same way I like snakes, Keeley concluded silently. She had little use for those who felt they could tell her how to behave, especially if it came from a man, and that included those of the cloth.

She and Attie leisurely consumed their coffee. Keeley felt closer to Attie now that Prue had shown just how dumb she could be at times. "Hawk Blackbean," she said. "Can you beat that?"

"Bet she's just using him," Attie said. Her face was low over her cup. "Prue just wants him to design the bell."

Keeley pondered Attie's words. "Maybe," she said slowly, "but she doesn't seem like somebody who'd use people. Maybe she really likes Hawk." It pained her to say it.

Attie stared at her with deadly concentration. "Why don't you offer to design the bell?"

"I break horses, Attie," Keeley said firmly. "That's what I do. Leave it to Hawk, if that's what Prue wants. Maybe he really can do a good job."

As they left, Prue called from behind the counter. "Hey, you two, I forgot to ask. The church is going to have a bake sale this Sunday. Right after services. Would you be willing to donate cookies or a pie or something? It's to raise money for the bell." She poured coffee for three customers as she spoke, never spilling a drop. "You men, too," she added, including them. "Ask your wives to send something if they would. It's for the good of the church and the town. Oh," she added as she set down the pot. "Keeley thinks the bell would be an excellent way to notify the town if there was a fire anywhere."

Several patrons glanced at Keeley. Bob Sabberd said, "Not a bad idea, Delaney." There were nods of agreement. She tipped her head slightly.

"What can you bring, Attie?" Prue asked.

Keeley saw Attie's eyes flare, then settle. "Peach pie, I guess."

"Thank you, Attie. I knew I could count on you. How about you, Keeley? Can you set up tables for us outside the church while service is going on, and then help sell afterward?" Prue's hands stayed busy, wiping the countertop, serving sweet buns, pouring coffee, seemingly very calm.

"Don't that woman ever sweat?" Attie whispered to

58

Keeley. Keeley frowned at her as Attie added, "And why ain't you being asked to bake?"

"Tomorrow. Don't forget. Right after church, twelve noon." Prue flipped her hand.

Keeley nodded. "I'll be there." Already she dreaded the thought of standing around a bunch of ladies who knew their place, a place that Keeley had never known and never wanted to. She and Attie climbed into the wagon and headed home.

"What makes her think that I'm the only one who bakes around here?" Attie asked. "Maybe I can't." She was furious and spittle flew from her mouth as she climbed onto the wagon. Keeley reached for the reins, and Addie grabbed them from her.

Keeley sighed tiredly and climbed up. "All right, Attie. I'll bake, and you set up the tables."

"I'll bake," Attie declared. "Otherwise you'll get sick all over again."

Keeley didn't argue, but Attie's comment made Keeley question again why she had gotten so sick and how she had come to lose the money.

They rode in silence all the way home.

Chapter Six

Even though she wore no hat, Keeley sweated in
the cool air. She wore clean pants and a plaid cotton
shirt. She had attempted to polish her boots to at
least a dull gleam. All those dresses swirling around
her with people coming and going in such nice clothes
as they bought cakes, cookies, pies, brownies, breads,
preserves and confectioneries left her feeling self-
conscious, but she vowed not to let it upset her.
Following Sunday service, Prue and two other ladies
helped with sales. They wore their Sunday finery:
frills on collars and cuffs, bonnets deep as shotgun

barrels, dresses of blue and yellow and green, long enough to cover soft, thin leather shoes.

Keeley watched the money grow in the cigar box. Actually, all that most of the women were doing was buying one another's donations and paying hard cash for them. They could have just swapped with each other, and it wouldn't have cost them anything. But then, the money was for the bell.

The Omaha bell was beginning to gnaw at Keeley's good humor. Broadsides had been plastered all over town announcing the bake sale. There was also a picture of the final design, drawn by Hawk Blackbean, tacked next to the posters. It was a nice thing that Prue was doing for Omaha, but why did she have to involve Blackbean? He was nothing but rattlesnake scum.

"I'll take this last cake, Miss Delaney." Lillian Pringle held out a silver dollar.

"That's twenty-five cents, Mrs. Pringle." Keeley reached into the box to make change.

"Oh, keep the whole dollar, Miss Delaney. Lord knows I can't afford it, but this town sure could use a fine bell."

Thanking her, Keeley handed her the lemon-frosted, triple-layered white cake. "The dish is Mrs. Natter's when you're finished with it, Mrs. Pringle. You have a good day, now." She tossed the coin into the box and listened to it clink heavily against the others.

Those who had traded with her had been respectful, probably because of Prue. Folks knew that Prue liked everybody no matter who they were, and out of respect for her, they were pleasant to Keeley. She was tickled, sensing their deeper, truer sentiments.

"That's it," Prue declared brightly. "There isn't a crumb left, and I promised Bob Solemn a piece of that lemon meringue pie I made. I was going to buy it for myself."

"I sold it, Prue," answered Mary Hahn. A buxom blond dressed in green, she had borne eight children who ran her ragged. "First thing."

"No matter," Prue said. "I'll make him another."

Nancy McGuire, a slight figure wearing a tailored blue dress, was busily counting the money. "Sixty-two dollars and five cents. Not bad."

Keeley agreed. "It's a start, for sure. Maybe you should hold a bake sale every week or so."

"I've thought about that," Mary said. "Would you help set up, Keeley? That's what makes it so success-ful. The tables are ready, and the food is waiting when people come out of church."

"And they're hungry," Nancy added. She wetted the tip of her finger and touched a cookie crumb lying on the table. Daintily, she put it in her mouth.

"I suppose we could if the weather's good," Prue said, eyeing the threatening but still dry sky. "We were lucky today."

"Set up inside," Keeley suggested, "before service starts, and have the food there too. The ladies could leave it on the tables as they come in. It'd sure add fine smells to the place."

"Make people's mouths water during service," Prue predicted.

Mary looked skeptical. "Think Reverend Barnes would go for it?"

"Only on rainy days," Prue said. "He likes the full attention of his flock."

"Is that why he screams at them?" Keeley asked.

She'd heard his loud, grating voice when she'd passed by the church on a few Sunday mornings.

"That's not screaming," Mary answered defensively. "He just gets excited about what he's saying, that's all."

"Sounds like screaming to me," Keeley insisted, resisting the urge to grin.

"Whatever," Prue said, adding a hearty chuckle. "Come now, ladies. Let's pack up and move these tables. Who owns what? Does anybody know?"

As she had done before, Keeley loaded the tables onto Attie's wagon, then delivered them to the list of loaners Prue had given her yesterday.

Still perturbed that Prue had assumed Attie would bake and Keeley would do the heavier work, Attie had refused to assist with sales, although Keeley had asked her at least a half-dozen times. Now Keeley was on her way home, dreading having to tell her sweetheart that she had suggested future bake sales. Likely, Prue would eventually have thought of the idea herself if Keeley had just kept her mouth shut, but she had been feeling good about people talking decently to her all morning. As much as she hated selling food, she'd just as soon have that other part happen again.

There followed a string of successful sales, all good money-makers until the last couple. By the middle of August, people were tiring of baked goods, and the women were beginning to grumble about the extra effort and money spent. Keeley continued to look for horses, returning home Saturday nights only because she had promised Prue she would help on Sundays and Attie had worked to bring their garden to the greatest fruition possible. Fortunately, the timing for the final bake sale was perfect. The $4,000 goal set to buy the bell had been met, not only by selling food, but also by donations from local businesses. Additionally, thick, gallon-sized glass jars were set on every store counter in town, including the saloons, which alone had garnered seven hundred dollars.

Having now raised the necessary funds and a little extra to boot, Omaha decided that it would have no one but Prue do the ordering of the bell. "Of course, I agreed," she later said to Keeley, relaying the conversation that had occurred at last week's post-church services. "But I asked them if it wouldn't be better if I personally went to the forge and ordered it to be sure they got it right. And do you know, Keeley, they agreed and authorized me to use whatever bell money I'd need for travel. I shall account for every penny I spend," she'd said. Her eyes had glowed, and her chest puffed up with enough pride to nearly pop the buttons off her calico dress as she spoke of their great trust in her.

Prue's costs were minimal. She traveled coach, ate shoebox lunches and stayed with her older sister and family while in Philadelphia. When she returned, she insisted that Bill Taylor publish her expenses in the *Omaha Penny Press* and to announce that the bell would be ready in two months. The townsfolk loved her the more, and her restaurant became busier than ever.

Keeley was considerably relieved that the bell

ordeal was finished and she was again free to roam the prairies looking for her prize racer. There were now five mustangs in her pasture; she hunted for another half-dozen or so. Now if only she hadn't ridden into Omaha yesterday to buy rope ... and to stop at Prue's.

Yesterday, she couldn't bring herself to tell Attie what she'd done this time. Now she had to. She sat with her head resting in her hands this morning while steam from her cup rose and bathed her face. Attie sat opposite her, idly stirring her coffee. Keeley tensed and said, "I gotta tell you something, Attie."

Attie's spoon stopped. She waited like she always did whenever Keeley began a conversation this way.

Keeley reached for the last piece of bacon lying on a platter between them. She started to bite it, then, absently holding it, leaned back and sighed. "I gotta go away for a while."

Attie remained mute, her eyes radiating worry.

"Ain't you gonna ask where?"

"Where?"

"Philadelphia, Pennsylvania."

"The bell," Attie said.

Keeley nodded. "It's ready."

Tight-lipped, Attie rose and began to clear the table, then poured water into the dishpan from the bucket by the fireplace. "When you leaving?" There was a catch in her voice that Keeley suffered for but did not respond to.

"Today. Two o'clock train."

Plates and cups clinked against the sides of the wash pan as Attie's hands swirled soapy water over them before dipping them into a second, smaller rinsing pan. "You going alone?"

Keeley had to strain to hear her. "I expect Prue will go. It's her bell."

"Did she ask Hawk Blackbean to go too? Everybody knows he's been sparking her lately."

"No." Keeley remembered the great relief she'd felt when she'd learned that only she and Prue would be going.

"Then, how do you come to be going, you a woman and all? Seems like she'd like to have a man along. Especially Blackbean with his big guns and sharp knife."

"I don't know," Keeley answered, feeling terrible remorse and discomfort for leaving Attie by herself. Seems she was always going off somewhere on her own and leaving sweet Attie alone to run the place. Last time she was a month away selling horses. Before that, three months trying to buy cheap mounts from all over the territory to train for the Army, thinking that it would be easier than trying to catch mustangs. And before that . . . Well, she'd been gone a lot over the two years that Attie had lived with her. "Maybe she don't feel comfortable traveling that far and that long with a man by her side that she don't know all that well."

"Oh, I'll bet she knows him, all right."

"Attie, I won't be having you speak poorly of Prue. She's a good woman, even if you don't think so."

"I don't!" The dishes stacked up as Attie slowly washed each one clean. She asked, "When did she ask you to go?"

Keeley had lied once to Attie and hated herself for it, and did still. She wasn't going to lie again. "She didn't ask me, Attie. I volunteered."

She heard Attie draw in a long, deep breath, saw

her body expand, her motions falter, listened to her slowly release her breath as though she were fighting for control. Keeley thought she probably was.

"You're mad at me, aren't you?" Keeley said.

"No, just disappointed, Keeley Delaney. You don't have a brain in your head, and you're blind as a bat."

Keeley refused to argue. "No matter. I'm going on Monday, and I'll be back in a week or two."

"Or two?" Attie finally faced her, drying her hands on the apron she wore.

"That allows for any mishaps along the way," Keeley said.

"Like what? You go to Pennsylvania, put a bell on a train, deliver it to Omaha and come home. One week is all it should take."

"It's four days one way, but if I'm wrong, I've allowed time, so you don't worry," Keeley said, trying to placate her.

"Oh, I won't worry, Keeley. But you better. You better worry about whether or not I'll be here when you get back."

Keeley was across the room in a flash and grabbed Attie to her breast. "What're you talking about? You ain't going anywhere. You stay right here, Attie Webster, and don't be making me worry about you while I'm gone. I'm going after a bell for this town —"

"A town you hate. You said so yourself."

"I promised Prue I'd help her bring it back, and I ain't going to break my word. Delaney words are as good as written contracts. We take pride in such."

Attie pushed her away. "Oh, you fool. If you could only hear yourself. Go on outside, and let me finish cleaning up in here. There must be something out

67

there that needs doing. Go do it!" She moved to the bed and began throwing quilted covers here and there. "Damn!" she cursed, as one of the blankets caught on the corner of the bedpost. She gave it a hard yank. There was the sound of ripping as the blanket gave way. "Damn you, Keeley. Now look what you've done. Go on now, leave me alone for a while."

Keeley all but slunk out of the soddy. Attie had no business talking to her that way. She strode to the barn and picked up a hammer and the sack of nails she'd bought weeks ago. She began working on the barn's west wall that should have been mended long ago. She attacked it with relish as she recalled her and Attie's earlier days when they had first met and the whole world turned magical. She slammed a few more nails into the wood and then sank to her knees, crying as she remembered how tender it had all been for them. Her little Attie, she thought, cared about Keeley a whole lot more than Keeley was ever worth. Streams of guilty tears flowed down her cheeks as her mind went back to that rainy fall day two years ago when Attie lived along the banks of the Missouri with her chickens flitting and pecking at the ground around that horse's hooves. Attie had been a bit scary then too.

Chapter Seven

When she was fifteen years old and wise beyond her years in the practical art of living, Attie Webster left her sod home five miles west of Fort Laramie, near Scotts Bluff, Nebraska. The fort, still active but now less so, was once heavily depended upon by wagon trains rolling toward Oregon and California. During Laramie's heyday, many a family had stopped to restock their supplies, trade weary oxen for refreshed teams, visit, learn the news, exchange gossip, marry, rest, gamble and look innocently and hopefully to the future. Transcontinental trains had curbed much of the post's business, but not all. It still bustled, but not enough to entice Attie Webster to remain and enjoy its busy but slow-growing population.

As she drove the rattletrap wagon, drawn by the family's only milk cow, Attie moved determinedly toward each morning's rising sun. Traveling alone, she covered nearly three hundred miles, having no destination in mind but advancing east and far from Laramie. She kept her days short, stopping where the grass was good and the water sweet and flowing, to generously rest the old cow.

Before her great move, she had been cook and housekeeper for her father, her mother having died when Attie was eight. Her father, already an old man when she was a toddler, unexpectedly died in bed one night. She left him to rot where he lay. He had been a lustful man, and she hated him. Dry-eyed and with malicious glee, she dug up the money she knew he kept stashed beneath a rock in the dirt floor of their crude soddy, an amount adding up to thirty-seven dollars. She stuffed the cash deep in a carpet bag, packing on top of it the Webster family Bible, a locket containing her mother's image and the remaining few pieces of china given to her mother on her wedding day long ago. With a hatpin she firmly anchored to her hair a once-beautiful straw hat flowered with a ring of dried daisies, which she could still see perched upon her mother's yellow hair.

Attie left the soddy without pausing to draw the door closed behind her. The coyotes would tend to her father. She needn't think further about him or her past life.

Eight weeks later when the wagon was barely

usable and the cow in dire need of stopping, Attie came to rest at the edge of the Missouri River. The sun shone bright and warm and the dark, fertile soil lay exposed along the riverbank. Rich, tall grass bent pleasantly beneath her bare feet surrounding her as far as the eye could see. Here, she could grow good, healthy crops.

She spent several days camping along the river and going into town to ask certain questions, particularly whether there was a fort anywhere nearby. Upon learning that there was, she went immediately to the Omaha land office to see what, if any, land was available at hand. She learned that there was a thirty-acre piece running along a section of river about five miles north of Omaha. There, for several miles, the Missouri ox-bowed so badly that severe flooding often occurred over that stretch each spring. She put a ten-dollar down payment on the land and signed the deed. Her X upon the mortgage guaranteed that she would pay ten dollars a month until the four-hundred-ninety-dollar balance was satisfied. That done, she went home to her property.

She lived in a small log house of oak, hickory and elm that she and a hired man, both working like mules, had constructed. Once that much was completed, she let him go and alone caulked logs, built a door, fireplace and chimney. She also made a small plank table, a dry sink and a bed of four short posts and bed-rope. A piece of tree trunk acted as a chair. Her greatest indulgence was in having purchased a halfway decent woodstove. Two dollars and twenty-seven cents remained from her original thirty-seven. She kept it carefully hidden at the base of a tree near the house in a John Mason canning jar that once had held peaches she'd bought in Omaha during a very weak moment.

She set up a laundry business in her new home, washing and ironing for the men in the fort. She used the old wagon, which she repeatedly repaired, and an old but sturdy horse she had purchased. She also did some townsfolks' laundry, worked from dawn until dusk seven days a week and never caught up.

She thought her life far better than that which she had previously known and believed she was fairly happy. She paid her mortgage on time and bought the things she needed. The rest she saved.

She worked as a laundress for three years. By then she was eighteen and already becoming bent with toil, her flesh dried out from the wind. Her skin had burned to a deep copper color, and her hair had grown very long. She refused all offers of marriage, believing she was better off a spinster. She was becoming known around Omaha as "Old Hat Webster" because of the battered straw bonnet with the faded clump of daisies attached to it, which she wore everywhere she went.

At that time, with her own family gone, Keeley Delaney was more alone than she had ever been in her life. Because of her parents' great drive to work their farm, she had socialized infrequently. Like many landowners, almost all of their energies went into farming and ranching, leaving little time to hobnob.

Keeley had long been aware of the lone woman living over on the Missouri, who was left undisturbed, she'd heard, because of her contentious ways. She was an old woman, some said. Others claimed she wasn't; she was just plain mean and never said much to anybody when she came to town. Keeley'd heard she had a half-wolf half-dog she never fed and kept vicious by repeated beatings.

Old Hat Webster didn't seem to be the sort that a body would care to visit, but Keeley was feeling unduly gloomy one dark, gray day. The slate-colored clouds hung so thick and low overhead she thought she might be able to reach up, snatch one from the sky and shake it so hard, it would dump its water all at once, creating her a good big pond. She could use a good big pond if she was to raise more horses. Meanwhile, her loneliness weighed down upon her more than all the rain clouds balanced up there in the thickening atmosphere.

She saddled Jingles and mounted up. She wore a raincoat and leather gloves as added protection against the increasingly cold wind that now blew Jingles' mane and tail nearly horizontal.

"I'm a crazy fool to be doing this on a day like today, Jingles," she shouted over the wind before dropping her voice to a mutter. When he nickered, she leaned over the saddle horn and patted him on the neck. "I could go to town. It's not so far as Old Hat Webster's, but I feel so glum today that only misery would accept my company." Becoming increasingly depressed as she headed east, she concluded, "That old woman sounds like she'd be about perfect to visit with. That is, if I don't get my leg bit off by her wolf" — somehow the dog-wolf had become pure wolf — "and my head ain't shot off." Old Hat had become a noted shooter, as well. "Probably taking my life in my hands by going over there, old horse, but today I just don't care."

Keeley hadn't seen another living soul in five weeks' time, staying to her farm, tending her large garden of potatoes, squash, carrots, lettuce, cauliflower and cabbage growing in soil she had plowed and dragged using Jingles. She'd hated every minute of it.

Despite being surrounded by a near-flat prairie and a sky that reached from horizon to horizon, she felt a trifle claustrophobic. It was the silence that was getting to her. She'd been without human contact long enough. Until this last year when Aaron had died, there'd always been somebody around. Now the only time she saw anybody was when she went to Omaha on business; even then the trips were brief with only minimal conversation.

It wasn't that she hated people. She just hated *these* people, the ones who hadn't come to her family's funerals. It never occurred to her until much later that they might not have known about the deaths until long after the fact, so little did the family associate with the town's citizenry. But mostly she believed they chose to ignore her family, never thinking to check otherwise. In Omaha, she knew she was still an unknown and seen as a little odd — somewhat like Old Hat Webster — just too stand-offish for her own good.

With her chin up, she rode on. She wanted to visit a body; she wasn't particular. Likely, Old Hat was so lonely, she'd be grateful for anybody's company.

It was nearing noon when she reined up before the log house. The building was set a good ways back from an oxbow, assuring its safety from spring flooding. Several large cottonwoods surrounded the place, affording it modest protection from the elements. Between the trees, clotheslines dripped with laundry. Close by, several crudely built benches held a number of large galvanized tubs catching rainwater. A three-sided, tin-roofed shed had been built against the east wall of the house. Beneath it were several brooding boxes for nesting chickens. A bay horse also enjoyed the shed's protection. A dozen hens huddled around the horse's hooves, busily pecking at the worn earth. Spotting Keeley, the bay nickered. Jingles snorted, and his ears came up.

Keeley shouted over the clatter of the storm, "Hello, the house!" She waited in the saddle, Jingles restlessly pawing the muddy earth and tossing water from his mane. The strong, gusty winds had shifted, blowing in from the north. Rain pelted her as she drew her hat low over her face. She waited another minute, then again shouted, "Hello, the house." She didn't relish the thought of turning back immediately after having come all this way, but she'd be willing to if Old Hat would at least give her a cup of coffee beforehand.

The plank door opened a crack. "What do you want?"

Keeley couldn't make out the face very well, but the voice didn't sound like that of an old woman.

"I come to visit."

"I don't visit. Leave your wash there by the door, and I'll have it for you in two days." The door closed.

"I ain't got no clothes to be washed," Keeley bellowed. "I wash 'em myself." After a bit, she added, "My ma taught me."

The downpour increased, banging even harder

against her and against Jingles' hide. Thick droplets pinged off the shed's roof. The chimney smoke was instantly blown away in tatters. "I said," Keeley yelled at the top of her voice, "I ain't got no clothes to wash, ma'am. I come to visit." Oh, how she wished she had a cup of coffee warming her hands and branding her insides clear down to her belly. She gave up, chucking to Jingles and reining him away. She took a final backward look at the door and drew in a sharp breath. A gun barrel protruded through the crack. Keeley threw up her hands. "Good God, woman. Don't shoot! I'm a female . . . and lonesome just like you. I just come to visit a bit, that's all. Put down that gun."

It seemed like years before the barrel disappeared and the door fully opened. A young woman stood in the shadows of the house. She wore the old hat Keeley had heard of and a plain, worn, brown linen dress. She was barefoot and apparently alone. So far, no wolf had appeared.

"Take off your hat," Old Hat ordered. "And keep your hands free of your sides."

Using both hands, Keeley slowly pulled off her hat and turned her head revealing her long hair pinned back in a bun. "I'm a woman, ma'am, that's all. Nothing dangerous. I ain't here to harm you. I'm not carrying a gun." She squinted as rain ran down her face so hard she could barely see.

"You just come to visit."

"That's all, ma'am."

"In the rain."

"Yes, ma'am."

"You stupid or something?"

"No, ma'am. Just lonesome to talk with somebody. Thought you might do."

"Why?"

Moving slowly, Keeley replaced her hat. Wiping her face with the sleeve of her raincoat did nothing but rub cold water across her skin. Her flesh crawled with a chill. "Ma'am, you gonna invite me in? If not, then I'll just go on back home."

The door opened wider. "What's your name?"

"Keeley Delaney. Live five miles west of here. Got my own place."

Old Hat Webster nodded. "I know who you are. Get down and come in. Put your horse in the shed."

Keeley dismounted. Beneath the shed, the bay warned Jingles away. Keeley loosened the cinch and looped the reins around the horn. "I'll not be long, old boy," she said patting his neck. "I'll have some coffee, and we'll just get on out of here. This is one cantankerous old woman. Or if she ain't old, and it don't look like she is, she surely will be in a couple more weeks, if she keeps on like she's doing right now. That old horse of hers ain't none too friendly either, is he?"

She removed her hat as she came into the house. A stream of water cascaded from the brim to the earthen floor. She looked up quickly, expecting to see the gun threatening her again, this time for her carelessness.

"I'm sorry, ma'am. I truly am." She faced a clothesline laden with drying laundry and ducked beneath it only to be confronted with another. She froze, waiting for directions from the woman.

"Never mind, Keeley Delaney. Make your way to the stove and back up to it. Get dry. Give me your coat. I'll hang it up for you."

"Yes, ma'am." Old Hat Webster didn't look to be much more than eighteen. As Keeley drew near the stove, she watched her hang the coat on a nail in the wall, then return to stand near the stove. Her shoulders were hunched a tad, and she carried herself as though she were bearing too heavy a burden. But she carried nothing. From a distance she could easily have been misjudged as elderly.

They were ringed by hanging laundry. The small bed in one corner and a tiny, rustic table were nearly lost to sight beneath the fibered jungle. Two empty washtubs were stacked near the dry sink. A pot of coffee smelling strong and delicious warmed on the stove. Keeley fought begging for a cup. A more mannerly woman would have offered her one sooner.

"Now, Miss Delaney, tell me why you came here on such a poor day as this." The woman pulled over the only chair, sat and folded her hands in her lap.

"Like I said, ma'am, I was looking for company. I thought with you living alone and all, you might be lonesome too."

"What makes you think I live alone?"

Keeley's face reddened. "Heard it someplace, I guess."

"I see."

The silence grew and thickened like molasses. Keeley sought for friendly words. She said, "It's nice to meet you all the same, Miss Webster." She wasn't going to call her Old Hat Webster, even though the bonnet on the woman's head was so bedraggled that the straw was frayed almost to the crown and the daisies had lost all their petals.

"I don't know if it's nice to meet you or not, Miss Delaney. I hope you're not looking for money, because there ain't none here. I'm a poor woman."

"Poor is all in how you see it, Miss Webster."

"Maybe so, Miss Delaney. Maybe so." Old Hat tipped her head downward, the bonnet's remaining tattered brim partially concealing her face. Keeley wished she'd remove the ragged thing so that she could get a good look at her eyes. She puzzled over why she wore it at all. "Do you drink coffee? Eat cornbread?" Old Hat asked.

"Yes, ma'am, I do." Keeley's mouth watered.

Old Hat rose and from a shelf near the dry sink, pulled down a covered tin. Inside was fresh, golden-yellow cornbread. She cut two large slabs and put them on ceramic plates. "Get us a couple of cups," she said, pointing to some hooks in the wall where three chipped white mugs hung.

Keeley removed two and put them on the table, ducking beneath laundry at every turn. She took it upon herself to pour coffee. From a stack of split wood in the corner, she selected a chunk and sat it on end. Carefully, she positioned her bottom upon it. Only seven or eight inches wide, it still made a fine stool.

Miss Webster offered a small dish of sugar. "I don't have any milk," she said without apology. "My cow died."

"Don't use sugar or milk, Miss Webster. But I thank you very much." Keeley took a swallow. The coffee was robust, sliding down her throat like good honey and scalding her from throat to belly. She emitted a contented *ahh.* "Good coffee, ma'am." She basked in the cabin's warmth, soaking up the heat of the rich drink and even enjoying Old Hat's mighty stand-offish company. Even concealed by her bonnet's slight shadow, Miss Webster's brown eyes were lovely, Keeley though

Keeley's cornbread disappeared quickly. Appreciatively, she licked the last of the crumbs from her lips. "You're a good baker, Miss Webster. My ma was too."

"My name is Attie, if you'd care to use it, Keeley Delaney."

Keeley smiled. "A pretty name if you ask me — Attie."

They said little for the next twenty minutes or so. Keeley wasn't good at chitchat, nor did she feel comfortable asking questions. She thought she might like to come back again one day, but for now she had stayed long enough. She returned the log to the wood stack and said, "I better be going. The rain ain't letting up, and I'd hate to have to cross a bad stream on my way home."

Attie nodded and handed Keeley her raincoat still sodden with moisture. Clenching her teeth, Keeley pulled it on, drawing it tight to her body. "It was real nice of you to have me visit, Attie."

"You don't talk a whole lot."

Keeley shrugged. "Sometimes I do."

"Come back sometime. Maybe you'll talk more next time." Attie pulled open the door. "I think I enjoyed your company."

"I just might do that, Attie. I like your company too."

"You ain't nearly as crazy as they say," Attie said dryly.

A tinge of anger slipped into Keeley's voice. "Didn't know anybody thought I was."

"Only those who don't know better. I'm sure they say the same about me, out here all by myself with only a wild wolf-dog."

"I didn't ever see your wolf, Attie," Keeley said, surprised that Attie knew what the town said about her.

"I don't have one. Never have. But if folks want to believe it, they will no matter what the truth is."

"They're wrong, Attie, about both of us." Keeley fetched Jingles and mounted up at the door. Attie smiled at her. "You look nice when you smile like that," Keeley said warmly. She looked beautiful, that's what she looked like. Keeley wanted to just sit in the saddle and stare at her even in the pouring down rain.

"You're getting wet, Keeley Delaney. Come back soon."

"I will, Attie." Attie could count on it, but Keeley didn't feel quite brave enough to tell her so.

Chapter Eight

Two weeks later Keeley returned to find Attie down by the riverbank, bending over the water, her dilapidated hat perched primly upon her head. The skirt of her faded blue sundress was efficiently tied around her waist and out of the way. She wore the sleeves rolled up, freeing her tanned, slim, muscular arms. She was busily washing several baskets of clothing brought over by horse and wagon.

It was nearing noon. The sky was clear, and the smell of new grass and strong lye soap filled the air.

Birds chirped hysterically. Attie quietly hummed a tune.

Keeley called out, "Howdy, Attie." Riding over, she dismounted, dropping Jingles' reins to the ground. His nose disappeared in the tall grass. "Didn't want to scare you," she said, smiling.

"I knew you were there a mile back," Attie answered with a grin. She sloshed a gray union suit in the river, then wrung it out before skillfully tossing it into a nearby tub of rinse water. From a basket beside her, she grabbed a white shirt, doused it in the river, rubbed lye soap on the heavily soiled elbows and collar, then vigorously scrubbed it clean against a large washboard. "I'm almost done here. Then we can go back to the house."

"Need any help?"

"Rinse those things in the tub, if you want, then throw them in that basket. I'll hang everything up back at the house."

Keeley doused while Attie scoured and scrubbed. "Men are so dirty," Attie said. Water splashed onto her face. Absently, she wiped it away with her arm and continued washing something brown against the board.

"Yep." Keeley grunted, squeezing water from a half-dozen socks at once. They sailed with a flourish into the basket.

They were done in thirty minutes or so. At the house, they hung the laundry, filling every line.

Attie stood back to admire their work. "A good day. I have to take a load back to the fort in a little while. Care to ride along?"

Keeley thought about that. Did she want to waste time riding on a wagon when she should be weeding and watering the garden? She supposed she could tie Jingles to the tailgate and ride as far as the gates, then go home from there. "I guess I could this once," she said, not really wanting to but reluctant to leave Attie so soon.

"I'll fix us some dinner real fast," Attie said, looking pleased as punch. Keeley followed her inside.

During the drive, they talked about land, cattle and crops. "I'd like to have a garden," Attie said. "But I'm too busy. I have a couple of tomato plants, and that's about it."

"What do you do in the winter with the laundry?" Keeley asked. "Gets pretty cold, don't it?"

Attie shifted the reins, saying, "I wash in the house. You saw what it looks like in there on a rainy day. It's an awful big mess. Then there's tubs sitting all over the place too. On clear days I can hang stuff outside, but they're just as likely to freeze as not. I snapped a sleeve off a blouse one time, it got so cold."

Keeley laughed heartily over the image. "What'd you do about it?"

"I sewed it back on and didn't charge for the washing. That woman was mad. She hasn't asked me to do any more laundry for her or her soldier husband." She clucked at the old horse who had begun to slow. "No matter. I got all the work I can handle right here."

"You like gardens, huh?"

"I had a garden years ago where I lived. I wasn't too bad at making things grow," she said pridefully.

"I hate raising crops," Keeley said with rancor. "All those stinking little weeds and worms and bugs. Just a whole lot of work with almost nothing to show for it."

84

"Maybe it's the way you grow the plants," Attie tactfully suggested. "What do you grow?"

Keeley shrugged. "Stuff. I'd rather grow horses."

"Then grow horses."

"But I have to grow a garden."

"Why?"

"My family always grew a garden. Mostly Ma did."

"Does she do it now?"

"My family's dead except for me, so now I have to do it."

"I'm asking you again, why?"

Keeley considered the question. "So I have vegetables to eat and food to can."

"And do you eat the food you grow? Do you put food by?"

It surprised Keeley to realize that the only thing she actually harvested were the potatoes and winter squash. The rest usually rotted in the field. "Not much of it I don't."

"Then buy your crops if you can afford it, and don't have a garden."

It was habit that drove Keeley to plant each spring. Hating the care it took her to maintain the plants, she let most die before they could produce. "I probably shouldn't have one. I suppose I still do because the Delaneys were always crop farmers."

Attie waved a pesky fly away from her face. "Do you like to cook?"

"Nope. Don't like to be inside much at all."

Conversation drifted while they competed to see who could spot the most meadowlarks, elk, rabbits and game birds. Attie won, and they laughed hysterically over whether the dead rabbit Attie saw alongside the road counted or not. "But a dead rabbit should be worth ten thousand points," Aggie argued. "You never see a dead rabbit. I should get extra points."

"A lazy coyote around here, that's all, Attie. Dead don't count." Keeley stood firm, and still laughing and clutching her sides, Attie yielded.

Before too long, Attie said, "I don't like doing laundry."

"Good money in it, ain't there?"

"If you have a big business, but the hours are long. I'm getting old before my time. I'm only eighteen and have this to look forward to." She thumbed the back of the wagon loaded with baskets of fresh laundry. "And look at my hands." She held them out for Keeley's inspection. "They look like they belong to somebody that's been dead for ten years."

"Oh, now, Attie, they ain't that bad." Keeley took one and gave it a general caressing. Attie's palms were thickly calloused, the backs rough and red. "Use more goose grease," she suggested, releasing Attie's hand. "What about getting married? Not so much laundry then, and somebody to look out for you all the time."

"Somebody to own me is more like it. I'll never get married. It's the same as slavery."

Keeley grunted. That's how she saw it. "Be some-body's housekeeper, then. That would be easier."

"I know," Attie said slowly, "but I could garden if things were different. I love to grow things, sure enough."

Thoughtfully, Keeley rubbed her jaw, staring at distant cotton-ball clouds. Her brows knitted as she said, "You're lucky that you got a home and a job already. I sure could use a hand out at my place. I couldn't pay anything, but they could have a garden and eat all they wanted. Maybe they'd be willing to put food by for the winter." Envisioning her spread, she smiled. "I got a real nice soddy. Pa built it solid and warm, but the barn's only fair and there ain't but one small tree nearby where my family's buried. Could plant more trees though. Trees need a lot of care."

Attie looked at her, her gaze lingering on Keeley's doleful face. "You're right, Keeley. You do talk a lot sometimes. I like it." She grinned lopsidedly, and Keeley's heart swelled.

Casting off her growing moodiness, Keeley asked, "What brought you to this area?"

Attie's smile faded. "I needed a better place to live, and this is where I found it."

"That's what my pa thought when he left Ohio years and years ago. He wanted his own land, so here we came. I was just a tyke then, I don't remember much of the ride."

"Do you get lonely?"

"I do," Keeley said. "Where's your family? Do you get lonesome?"

"Some days," Attie answered. "My folks are dead. But I don't mind being by myself. Most of the time, anyway. I've got used to it."

"Too bad I didn't catch up with you sooner and hire you on." Keeley laughed generously and not at all seriously. "I think we would have done good together. But I couldn't pay you, anyway."

"I thought about it some already, Keeley. You wouldn't have to pay me anything. Not if I could grow a garden and have a decent place to live. I could make money selling vegetables to the fort and in town — if you'd allow it, and you'd get whatever we thought was fair to you."

Keeley felt her head swell as though she had just

inhaled a wagonload of hayseed. Her vision blurred for a brief moment. Suddenly, she wasn't at all certain that she wanted someone else in her house. Lonely though it became from time to time, especially during gloomy days and long winter months, she had come to enjoy her own company. She didn't bump into anyone else, didn't have to consider others' feelings or ask permission to do something. She didn't have to do one blamed thing she didn't want to, including getting up early every morning — which she sometimes didn't.

"What do you think of the idea, Keeley?"

Attie's question pierced her thoughts. What did she think about it? She didn't know.

Attie regarded her for a long moment. "Guess you were just talking, huh? Thought you might have been serious."

"But what about your house, Attie?"

"Keep it, I guess. I don't think I can sell it because of the oxbow so close and the flooding every spring."

Then why not have Attie move in with her? Keeley asked herself. She *was* lonely, if only she'd admit it, and getting up late in the mornings depressed the hell out of her, made her hate the rest of the day. Maybe Attie would cook for them both. Maybe there would be profit in raising crops if they truly worked at it. "How do you feel about cooking?" she asked.

"I'd love to cook for you, Keeley. It would make me proud."

"Stop the wagon, Attie." Attie did, looking scared and worried at the same time. "Don't be fretting," Keeley said, patting her arm. She jumped from the wagon and untied Jingles from the tailgate. Mounting up, she said, "I'll be back to your house in two weeks.

You be packed, and I'll take you to my home. I believe you'll be a fine addition to that old farm." Now that she had committed herself, Keeley felt wonderful about the whole idea.

"I'll be ready," Attie said.

Keeley whirled Jingles away and galloped westward toward her farm, yelling "Yahoo!" to the sky. She felt good. She felt *damn* good. Attie was coming to live with her. She'd start tidying up the place today. "Yahoo!" she yelled again.

Chapter Nine

Keeley's mind reeled with confusion as she dropped the sack of nails she had been holding and set aside the hammer. Attie was as important to her as was breathing, yet there was this inexplicable and terrible strong pull toward Prue against which she constantly battled. Attie could see through Keeley as though she were glass. She didn't know what to do, other than to go to Philadelphia as she had promised and help Prue bring back the bell. If she hadn't given her word, she'd stay for Attie's sake, but a Delaney promise was supposed to mean something.

At eleven she and Attie had a silent dinner, after which Keeley packed to leave for the two P.M. train. "Will you drive me there?" she asked the stewing Attie.

"Not on your life, Keeley Delaney." Attie busied herself at the sink.

"What about Jingles? If I ride him, he'll need to be brought back. I can't afford to board him for two weeks. It's a half-dollar a day!"

"I thought you said you'd only be gone a little over one." Attie's dishcloth swiped the table in wide, angry circles.

"I told you, Attie, I might have to be gone up to two weeks. I'm hoping not."

"Well, I'm sure you'll figure out something." Attie continued briskly straightening the already tidy soddy.

Keeley paused at the door. Her small carpetbag contained extra clothing and three shoebox lunches for the trip ahead. She waited for Attie to stop moving about. When she didn't, Keeley said, "Well, then, I got to go. I'll see you soon." As she stepped up to Attie to kiss her, Attie turned away, leaving Keeley only a cool cheek upon which to leave her final affection. Angrily, she said, "You're a damn stubborn woman, Miss Attie."

She simmered all the way to Omaha, resenting that she'd have to stable Jingles. This was an expense she hadn't counted on.

The hundred dollars she had won during the race was now down to eighty-seven, what with having lost some of the winnings in the mud the day of the fight and the supplies they'd bought since then. Playing it safe for the trip, she tucked fifty dollars deep into her pants pocket. That would be plenty for coach and meals. Likely, they'd stay at Prue's sister's. The remaining money she left with Attie, who now stored both their earnings in her John Mason canning jar hidden deep in the foot of their corn-shuck mattress.

Keeley fervently wished the gold from the sale of her remuda was in that jar too. She often dwelled upon who had robbed her and how the switch from gold pieces to stones had been made without her knowledge. She'd been so sick she'd slept right through the theft without knowing it. But wouldn't Jingles have made some noise if a stranger came near? Not if the man was damn good with horses — and knew she was sick. Hawk Blackbean? What would Blackbean want with her piddling little money? He was a top rancher and richer than most ranchers in the area. He was actually a smart businessman, however uncouth and distrusted by others. Besides, he didn't know she was going.

She moaned aloud as she rode, telling Jingles, "I'm giving myself a bad headache, old boy, with all this thinking. I sure wish you could talk, and I wish Sheriff Butts could have done something."

Butts had, but it had been little. She reported her loss the day after she arrived home, and Butts sent his deputy to investigate. The paymaster at Fort Niobrara could give him no information, and the trail that Keeley had traveled was dead cold.

She turned her mind toward seeing Prue, refusing to waste further time feeling woeful about anything. Attie had made her point. Keeley vowed she would do nothing that would make her ashamed to come home. Anyhow, what could she do? Prue was a woman, and women didn't go around sparking other women — except for when Keeley had sparked Attie. But that had been different. She and Attie had sparked each other.

She stabled Jingles and went to the restaurant. Prue was waiting, bubbling and enthusiastic. She wore a pink skirt and white blouse and bonnet. Two carpetbags sat by the door.

Prue's eyes flashed as she snatched up the luggage. "I'm so excited I can hardly stand it," she told Keeley. "You take care, Timmy. I'll be back as soon as I can. "Bye, all."

Timmy and several customers wished her good luck as she and Keeley left, the doorbell jangling behind them. "Everything'll be fine, Miss Prue," Timmy called. "You have a good time."

Prue led them to the station at the north end of town. At the loading platform, she dropped her bags and checked her watch. "Twenty minutes. I've already got our tickets. I bought them yesterday to save some time. You can pay me back on the train." She was breathless, and her eyes glowed as she stared westward. "Ought to hear the whistle any minute now." Pleased with her thoughtfulness, Keeley thanked her for her foresight.

The train ground into the station on time. People debarked or boarded. Down by the freight cars, drays were maneuvered into position as the doors rolled open to receive or disperse goods. Business was conducted with great efficiency, and the train was almost ready to leave again.

From the platform Keeley studied the closest of three third-class coaches through its opened windows. Two rows of wooden seats were separated by a narrow aisle. There was a primitive comfort room on one end, the odors of which she could smell, and a small woodstove at the other. Along the walls were several globed oil lamps. Tired people looking dreadfully cramped and uncomfortable stared at her with dull eyes. Some folks were eating, likely out of food baskets they carried; exhausted mothers held weeping and sleeping children; men hid behind newspapers.

Keeley shuddered, sighing with resignation. The next four days were going to be awful.

"This way, ladies," the porter said and picked up Prue's baggage.

Surprisingly, he bypassed the coaches, smoking, cook, dining and parlor cars before coming to the first of two Pullman sleeping cars, beyond which were the freight and baggage cars.

"Here you are." Still carrying Prue's luggage, he assisted her up the portable steps. Following them, Keeley stared as she entered the sleeper. The car's interior was finished in shining inlaid woods and marquetry. Deep blue velvet drapes covered individual sleeping areas. Plate-glass mirrors on the car doors and ornate lighting fixtures overhead added to the heavy opulence. The porter stopped midway down the car. "These will be your compartments," he said, setting their luggage on the lower of two narrow bunks made up with snowy-white linen and fine soft-blue wool blankets on thick mattresses. "If you have any questions, please ring the bell." He pointed to a yellow, silken cord hanging by their beds. Respectfully, he tipped his hat, accepting a small tip from Prue, and left.

Dazzled by the car's elegance, Keeley asked, "You sure this is ours, Prue? Ain't we supposed to be up in coach?" She removed her hat, craning her neck in all directions.

"This is ours," Prue answered cheerfully, energetically throwing Keeley's bag on the upper bunk and pushing aside her own. She kicked off her shoes and stretched out on the lower bunk. No sooner had she settled than she was up again. "Quick," she said breathlessly. "Let's go to the parlor and get a seat by a window." She was on her way before Keeley could argue.

The car was quickly filling, but Prue did manage to get a window seat and promptly sat down on a small, purple velvet couch.

Keeley joined her, still gaping at her surroundings. The parlor car was equally as lavish as the sleeper, with plush couches and chairs covered in dark velvets, windows draped with white lace curtains, ornate brass lighting fixtures, thick Oriental floor rugs, small round tables sitting here and there. Bewildered by such elegance, Keeley closed her eyes. If she had one-tenth of the money it took to outfit this car —

Prue drew aside delicate lace drapery. "Look, Keeley. There's Hawk Blackbean. I told him we were leaving today. I'll be right back." She rapped a small fist against the pane, catching his attention, then hurried from the car.

"Oh, Jingles," Keeley said to the horse on whose back she wished she now were instead of slumped down on this couch and watching Prue hurry toward Blackbean. "I am in big trouble. I can't even guess what this is gonna cost me." She was angry that she hadn't been consulted about how she would like to travel. She saw her money slipping through her fingers like sand through a sieve. She was angrier still when Hawk Blackbean gave Prue a hug, and Prue let him, before heading back to the car. She cursed, squeezing tighter the edges of the seat she was already gripping.

The sun caught Prue's smooth skin, sending flares of light across her face as she rejoined Keeley. "He's such a nice man." Keeley nearly drew blood, biting her tongue to keep from saying something she would regret. "Now, about your ticket, Keeley. You don't mind, do you? I knew you wouldn't want to travel all the way to Philadelphia third class. I know I certainly wouldn't."

That was twice now that Prue had been wrong. She didn't know the truth about Hawk Blackbean, and she sure didn't know Keeley very well. Uncomfortable though it would be, third class would have suited her just fine.

"It comes to one hundred and seventy-five dollars, round trip." Prue held out her palm, her face beaming. "This way, we won't have to think about it anymore."

Keeley sat up straight. "Prue," she whispered, barely able to speak at all. "I don't have that kind of money. I . . . I . . ." Her voice trailed off as she stared unblinking into Prue's smiling eyes. Prue was asking for a *fortune*!

"Well, no matter, Keeley," she said a bit stiffly. "You can pay me back when you get it. I just thought that when you agreed to come with me, you could afford it."

"Why didn't you check first?" Keeley worked to discipline her voice, to maintain control and not scream at Prue.

"You sold a bunch of horses in Niobrara, didn't you? I thought you had plenty."

"The money was stolen. Every bit of it."

Prue's fingers flew to her mouth, and for several seconds she sat still as a post. Keeley watched her eyes. They never flickered as she appeared to contemplate this revelation. "All right, then," Prue pronounced decisively. "We'll do the best we can. I'll pay your way. You do what you can, when you can. I know I can trust you."

Keeley knew that Prue wouldn't starve if she weren't paid immediately. Prue once told Keeley that she had come to town with a small inheritance from her father's death, determined to open a fine food eatery. She had, and made a modest living from it. She wasn't rich, but she wasn't uncomfortable either. But Keeley certainly was. "I'll switch to a coach seat," she offered, still fighting for composure.

"It's too late for that. Your berth is already paid for."

"Damn." Sweat built upon Keeley's brow.

"Now, never mind, Keeley. We'll work it out. We're friends, aren't we?" Prue's eyes seemed to beg Keeley not to be angry with her. Keeley was trying not to be. But how would she explain to Attie that she needed the rest of their money to pay back Prue? "Let's just forget about it for now and sit back and enjoy the trip."

And just how, Keeley puzzled, was she to go about doing that? Instantly, she was broke, and the train hadn't even pulled out of the station yet. And there was Prue already acting like nothing was wrong as she turned and grinned once more like a fool at Hawk Blackbean, the man who wanted to kill Keeley not so long ago. "This is bad for me, Prue," she muttered unhappily.

"It was either traveling first class, Keeley," Prue

said firmly, her eyes never leaving the window, "or subjecting ourselves to the possibility of catching chills, a sick headache, a sore throat or . . ." She leaned toward Keeley and whispered, ". . . even getting diarrhea. But worse still would be getting Influenza." She shuddered as she mentioned the disease.

Keeley could only trust that Prue knew what she was talking about and therefore justified in buying the more expensive tickets. Her words had scared Keeley a trifle. Maybe her reasoning would help Keeley explain things to Attie.

She sank low on the couch, her legs stretched out before her, and began to snooze. She had often found sleep a great way to escape difficulties.

"Not here, Keeley. Come on, we'll both take naps."

The train started out as they returned to their compartment. Soon, Keeley lay sound asleep, dodging thoughts about the mess she was in.

She awoke with Prue standing on the edge of the lower bunk wiping sweat from her brow with a scented lace handkerchief. "You've been having a bad dream, Keeley."

Pleasant odors of bath salts wafted from Prue's body. Keeley wanted to reach over and grab her. Instead, she slowly sat up to avoid knocking her head against the ceiling. "Where are we?" It was dark outside; nothing showed in the window but her own reflection given off by the gas lamps apparently lighted some time ago.

"We're near Des Moines." Prue stepped to the floor.

"Where's that?"

"In the middle of the state of Iowa. I expect we'll

make a brief stop there and then continue on. Want to get off for a while? It's a big city."

"I'm not getting off this train until we get to Philadelphia," Keeley declared. "There's gonna be too many people. I can't believe we've come this far. Pa said it took weeks when we moved here."

"Oxen . . . wagon," Prue answered simply.

Keeley wiped her hands across her face and slid from her berth. She retrieved her hat from the floor where it had fallen while she slept and sat beside Prue on the lower bunk. "Times sure do change, don't they?"

"Times change, and so do people. Nothing stays the same."

"Put that way, it sounds like a mighty melancholy thought, Prue. Change is supposed to be good, you know." Keeley tossed her hat back onto her bed.

"I know, but it isn't always. Big city changes are awful. Tearing down buildings, tearing up streets. I came west to get away from all that. It's also why I work so hard at church and at the social events the town puts on. I like change where things are certain to become better. And if I'm involved, I can have a voice in how those changes happen."

"You sound like a politician," Keeley said ruefully.

Prue's smile widened until her face shone. "Anyway, take you, Miss Keeley," she said, putting that burning hand of hers on Keeley's sleeve. "You are the most different person I know. A real change from what I'm used to or have ever known, and that's good for me."

"How's that?" Keeley shifted to better see Prue's face.

"Well, first off, I've never known a woman to dress as a man. And I've been told you wear a gun sometimes too. That's what I call different." They conversed softly, drawing in their feet as others made their way along the restrictive corridor.

"I call it being comfortable," Keeley answered. "Ma had me in my dress on Sundays when she was alive, but I don't wear it anymore."

"Not even out of respect for her memory?"

"Can't," Keeley explained. "I can't afford to go around all gussied up even for a day's time. I got to be out working, doing things that don't allow me to be wearing a dress." She paused. "It's a nice thought, though. I didn't mind doing it for Ma, but I actually hate wearing the cumbersome thing."

"You see?" Prue replied, shifting closer to Keeley's side. "That's another thing I like about you. You're so honest and pure of heart."

"You sound like you been reading too much poetry," Keeley said, feeling her face turn crimson.

Prue leaned over and kissed Keeley's burning cheek. "You are a poem, Keeley. A poem of prairies and big skies, fast horses and clean living. I think you're the nicest lady I know."

At a late supper, Prue ate a chef's salad and sipped hot cinnamon-flavored tea. She stirred her drink with the cinnamon stick and chatted nonstop about the bell and how comfortable they were with their first-class accommodations.

"How do they keep the food fresh?" Keeley asked, spearing a bite of buffalo tongue.

"It's stored in big iceboxes in the baggage cars," Prue replied.

"Hmm, who would have thought it?" Keeley stuffed herself with green turtle, buffalo tongue, loin of beef, sweetbreads, baked sweet potatoes, English plum pudding in brandy sauce and Neapolitan cream with coffee. She paid seventy-five cents for her meal and thought she was being robbed.

After using the comfort station and parking her boots beneath Prue's bed, she climbed heavily into her berth and drew the night curtain. In the privacy of the cramped confines, she struggled out of her clothing and into a white cotton nightgown. She gave her pants, shirt and hat a kick toward the end of the bunk, then flopped back and lay like a sodden log. Sweating heavily in the tight quarters, her stomach ached, her ears rang and her heart longed for home. Below her lay Prue still chatting about the day and their wonderful supper. A single moan was emitted from Keeley's bone-dry mouth before she fell into a deep sleep.

She awoke to the rocking of the train and its monotonous clacking as the wheels rode the rails. Lamplight filtered through a gap in her curtain. She wasn't sure what had disturbed her, and she lay quietly, desperately trying to return to sleep and oblivion. She was almost out when she felt warm breath upon her cheek. Thinking danger, she quickly sat up, banging her head against the ceiling. "Ow!" she barked.

"Shh. You'll wake people up." Prue stood on the lower berth, her head and shoulders poking beneath Keeley's curtain.

Rubbing her skull, Keeley bent close to her, whispering, "What's wrong?"

"Nothing. I just couldn't sleep and wondered if you could."

"Yes," Keeley answered strongly. "Always."

"Can I come up?"

"*Here*? *Now*?"

"Yes."

"What for?" she whispered again, her words much closer to a panicky hiss, even to her own ears. "Why don't we just switch berths? I don't mind sleeping down there."

"Oh, don't be silly. There's plenty of room. I'm cold, and I'm forlorn, so move over, and let me come up."

Keeley rammed her body against the wall. Prue climbed in and tightly snuggled against her before drawing up the blanket. "See? I told you there was lots of room."

Keeley didn't think so. She thought she might melt from the heat too. Prue slid her arms around Keeley's neck and waist and, like a kitten, purred against her neck. Keeley didn't dare move. Not one muscle. She barely allowed herself a decent breath. When she exhaled, she'd likely hit Prue right in the face. She lay stiff and frozen, her heart thundering, her body wanting to rise up and run like the devil was after her.

Prue began to stroke Keeley's back, slowly up to her neck, then all the way down to her hips. Keeley gritted her teeth. The sensation was powerful, feeling much like the savage thunderstorms that rolled across the Nebraska prairies with boiling lightning strikes that shattered trees into matchsticks along the Missouri. She emitted a groan, biting her lower lip in an effort to stop herself.

"Prue," she murdered through locked teeth. "It's nice and all, but I think it's time you stopped."

"Why?" More purring. More hot breaths against Keeley's neck.

"I can't sleep."

"All right." Prue pulled away her hand and began to softly run her palm over Keeley's chest. "Mmm, my, you are small here, aren't you?"

Keeley clutched Prue's wrist. "Prue, I can't sleep when you do that to me."

"You're not supposed to, Keeley. You're just supposed to be very quiet, not breathe too loudly, not shout, not talk."

"This is hard on me, Prue." Keeley was trying to remain the strong person Prue had just asked for, but she might as well have asked Keeley to lasso the moon. She couldn't do either.

"All right, then, Keeley, you sweet thing. Sleep well, and I'll see you in the morning." Prue kissed Keeley on the cheek and slipped back down into her own bed.

Keeley slept only fitfully during the next three nights, worried — no, scared — that Prue would climb into bed with her again. How much strength did the woman think Keeley had? Her anger also brewed because so far, only she had paid for their meals. Additionally, during their final night aboard the train before reaching Philadelphia, Prue dropped yet another unpleasant surprise.

Keeley had been nearly asleep, only half listening to Prue's nightly monologue, when she announced, "We'll take a hotel tomorrow night while they load the bell, and you can relax there."

"Hotel? What hotel? I don't have money for a

hotel!" Keeley was instantly awake and alert, seeing more of her cash pouring from her pockets as though there were gaping holes in each.

"Calm down, Keeley," Prue said. "They aren't that expensive, and we'll only be staying one night. You can pay me back."

Keeley moved aside her curtain and looked over the edge of her bed. "No! I don't take money from women. I don't take money from *any*body. Delaneys ain't like that. I'm giving you ten dollars in the morning, right off. It's bad enough I already owe you for the train ticket, but it'll be a start toward what I owe you. And I'll be giving you ten each month after this." She was near panic. "Damn, I thought we'd be staying at your sister's. I remember you have a sister. It said so in the *Omaha*." Now she'd have to have a bigger garden to make that kind of money. Horses just took too long to get ready for sale.

Prue peeked up at her. "Oh, Keeley. You worry too much, dear. You must learn to enjoy life more. Staying at my sister's would be so boring. All those children of hers running around and causing a ruckus, when I just want to rest and get back home with the bell." She got out of bed and kissed Keeley's cheek, then, more gently, Keeley's mouth. Keeley remained unmoving, not knowing what to do, other than nothing, until Prue lay back down again, which, thank God, was instantly.

Chapter Ten

The following morning with baggage in hand, Keeley, whose mouth hung open as she stared at the high, sprawling station, followed Prue at a brisk pace. Hissing trains seemed to be impatiently waiting to move onward; multitudes, from well-dressed people to those in nothing but rags, rushed by; porters in bright red caps as well as dirty little boys and unkempt men offered to carry their luggage for a small fee; smoke shops packed with newspapers and tobacco products, inter- spersed amongst the small cafes that smelled of coffee and frying meat, lined both sides of the station's walls.

Before going to their hotel, Prue insisted on checking upon the bell's whereabouts. She spoke to a freight agent through a barred window while nearby, Keeley waited on a wood bench, staring at the overwhelming edifice surrounding her. Great pillars held up the structure. Everything had been painted a base gray. Placards advertising every possible event and happening in Philadelphia, plastered the columns. Keeley read a sign six months old advertising a cricket game. She had no idea what a cricket game was. She read another regarding a symphony. Again she did not understand. Soon, Prue was at her side.

"Everything's in order. They'll load the bell early tomorrow morning."

A huge weight lifted from Keeley's shoulders as they exited the station, but once outside, the oppressive sensation again returned. She ogled Philadelphia, intimidated by its tall buildings and numberless people. There was so little earth, so much smoke. "Where's the dogs and cats?" If she could have seen but one dog or cat, she would have felt better — safer. Dogs and cats were normal.

Several carriages waited at the curb. A mutton-whiskered driver dressed in a black suit nimbly leaped from the driver's seat of a covered, four-wheeled coach and landed directly in front of Prue. "Where to, miss?" He took her bag, carefully placing it in the carriage. Keeley watched opened-mouthed as Prue willingly gave up her luggage to a complete stranger.

"The Brewster Hotel on Court Avenue," she said as he aided her onto the seat. He reached for Keeley's satchel.

"I'll carry my own." She clung to her bag with both hands.

"Suit yourself, mister." The cabbie climbed onto the seat and took up the reins of a team of blacks.

"And I ain't no mister," she growled as she sat beside Prue, who was busily adjusting her tan dress and petticoats. "I'm a woman." She thought she heard the driver snicker, but she wasn't sure and let it go.

The city's grandeur overpowered Keeley with its many wall-to-wall stone, wood or brick structures she witnessed during their hasty ride to the hotel. Philadelphia swarmed with life as carriages and wagons of all types and descriptions clattered by. People filled the sidewalks; angry, shouting men yelled at unruly horses or at other drivers, as they negotiated the narrower thoroughfares. In high-pitched voices, boys hawked newspapers; neighbors called to each other through opened windows; horseshoes rang in uneven rhythm against cobblestone surfaces.

Keeley and Prue were delivered sharply to their destination, and a blue-uniformed bellhop led them to a third-floor suite. Keeley, whose heart was still pounding wildly from the elevator ride, tripped on a thick, green carpet as she entered their large room. Oak-framed mirrors hung against light green flowered wallpaper; gaslight fixtures more ornate than most flowers she had seen were spaced around the room; two large shining brass beds, each made up with blood-red covers and white linen, were separated by an ornate cherry nightstand covered with a large, white doily upon which sat a tall oil lamp of pink glass.

She set her bag on one of the beds and wandered over to the lace-curtained window. Carefully drawing aside one panel of the frilly drapery, she gazed at the congested street below while Prue claimed the second bed and efficiently began emptying her luggage.

"This is a wondrous city, Prue," Keeley said. "But I wouldn't want to live here. I couldn't live here."

Prue shook several items free of wrinkles before hanging each in a wardrobe. She closed the door and glanced Keeley's way. "Your mouth is hanging open, Miss Keeley."

Keeley snapped it shut.

"Listen," Prue said brightly. "We've still got the afternoon to do something with. Let's go to the zoo, or see a play or a museum. And there's art and science. The Liberty Bell is here. There's ballet, opera, a huge library —"

"Stop!" Keeley put up a hand. She felt overwhelmed and unable to think. Making a decision, even a small one, seemed impossible. "I'm going to take a nap," she said. "Then I'm going to eat supper. Then I'm going to bed for the rest of the night. That's what I'm going to do." She stood fast, her chin thrust mulishly forward.

Prue's eyes sparkled. "Ever heard of Betsy Ross? Her flag is here."

"No, I never heard of her, and I don't care what she's got here. I'm tired, and I'm not moving from this room until I have to."

Prue exhaled heavily. "You should. There's more to life than Omaha."

Keeley scowled darkly. "There ain't even Omaha as far as I'm concerned." She felt like she was being pushed from pillar to post by somebody who was tying her head in knots, in a city that had too much in it. And for what? So that she, Keeley, could ride back from Philadelphia escorting a big, bronze bell that she really didn't give a hoot about? Her life was not going well, and she wanted to go home.

Some of the light seemed to fade from Prue's eyes. "All right, Keeley. Have it your way, but you'll miss some beautiful things."

And it would probably cost plenty to see them. Keeley had spent all she was going to except for food, and that, she was sure, was going to be far too much. She looked again at the buzzing thoroughfare below. She was breathing heavily having stood up to Prue, not an easy thing to do against one who seemed to bend Keeley to her whim as though she were made of a thin piece of copper wire.

Her unhappiness increased during supper in the hotel's splendid dining hall. Nevertheless, she, and Prue, too, ate succulent chicken cordon bleu and strawberry shortcake out of season. They sat at a small table covered with white linen and ate from china using silver utensils. She continued wearing her men's garb, albeit clean and neatly pressed, with no plans in her future to wear women's clothing. She was assumed to be a man in spite of her hair hanging free to her shoulders, and as such was handed the check at dinner's end. She looked questioningly at Prue as the waiter walked away.

Prue smiled with amusement. Her eyes twinkled as she said, "What did you expect, Mr. Delaney? They don't see women dressed like men here, any more than they do in Omaha. Leave the check and the money on the table, and let's go back to the room." She touched a linen napkin to the corners of her mouth and rose.

Keeley looked at the bill, and her eyes grew large. She whispered, "But it's ten dollars and ten cents. I can't leave that kind of money just lying here."

Prue picked up her handbag from the table. "Of course, you can. It's done all the time." She waited as Keeley, frowning doubtfully, dug into her pocket. Her hands shook as she laid the cash beside the bill.

"Leave an extra twenty-five cents for a tip," Prue suggested.

"What for?" Keeley sputtered, glancing at other diners who appeared quite at ease with themselves, as though they ate here seven nights a week.

"Because it's the polite thing to do," Prue answered quietly. "It's for the waiter who took care of our table."

Keeley laid down a quarter. "Doesn't he get paid?" she asked as they left the dining room.

"Yes, but this is to tell him what a nice job he did and that we appreciate it."

Keeley didn't appreciate it. It was her money he was taking for doing something he was already being paid to do. "Stupid," she grumbled. She still had sixteen dollars and fourteen cents left following this meal and having already paid her share of the room's cost. But she didn't want to waste even a penny for something as foolish as a tip.

On their way back upstairs, Keeley consoled herself by planning on subtracting Prue's cost of her dinner and half the tip from what she owed her. She even managed to partially enjoy the elevator ride up to their floor.

Not long after, Keeley lay in her nightgown, cool and relaxed beneath the bedsheet. There was nothing she could do about her problems right now. The room

110

was dark. Heavy green velvet night drapes were pulled across the window. Shadows loomed large and unfamiliar. Keeley heard Prue's sheets rustle, followed by a light footstep. Without a word, Prue crawled in beside her. Keeley sat bolt upright. "Prue, what are you doing?"

"I'm going to sleep with you."

Keeley shifted away from her body, already pressing against hers, and the arms that were reaching for her. "*Why?*"

"Because I like you, and I know you like me too. I see it in your eyes all the time."

Playfully, Prue giggled and tugged at Keeley's waist. Keeley remained rigidly seated. "Prue, this ain't right. It ain't right at all."

"Why don't you lie down beside me while you explain?"

Keeley sweated and considered it. Attie would kill her if she knew Prue was in bed with her. But Attie wasn't here, and Attie was awfully mad at her. Keeley lingered a bit longer before deciding that lying next to Prue was more friendly than thinking about Attie arguing with her just before Keeley left. She lay back down.

"There, that's better," Prue said, lightly touching Keeley's hair. "Can you explain it to me, Keeley?"

"Explain what?" She couldn't even remember what the question had been.

"Why it isn't right for me to lie next to you."

Oh, yes, that was it. Keeley squeezed her eyes shut, facing the truth. It was because of Attie. How could she explain to Prue about Attie? She didn't ever want to hurt her Attie. If she did something with Prue, she'd have to confess or die of guilt and shame.

That would make Attie feel terrible. Maybe she'd even leave Keeley, if she hadn't already, which Keeley prayed hadn't happened.

"Why isn't it right, Keeley? You do care for me, don't you?"

Prue's body smelled of some intoxicating fragrance that Keeley didn't recognize. She felt so soft against Keeley's side with her arm lying across Keeley's chest and her knee resting over Keeley's thigh. It made Keeley ask herself why lying next to Prue would be wrong. Keeley wasn't Attie's husband or anything like that. For that matter, they'd never even told each other they loved each other. Did that mean Keeley wasn't all that attached to Attie? Did it, then, make it all right for her to actually love another woman? Touch another woman? She supposed it did. "I guess it's all right, Prue. I just wasn't thinking."

"And now you are."

"I guess."

"Then may I kiss you?"

Kiss me? But Keeley made no effort to stop her. Prue's mouth was softer than Attie's, and larger. Attie used her tongue, but not much. Right now, Prue was all over the inside of Keeley's mouth. And then here came Prue's hand beneath Keeley's gown. Keeley forgot all about her worries as Prue slowly worked Keeley's gown above her breasts before caressing Keeley's skin from shoulder to knee. Keeley could only manage to breathe. She felt her body relax and her bones melt into the mattress. Prue sat up and removed her own nightgown. She pulled Keeley's from her, then lay full-length on top of her.

Keeley slid her arms around Prue and held her tightly as Prue nestled between Keeley's thighs. She began to play with Keeley's nipples using her lips and tongue, pulling on Keeley and caressing her with long damp strokes across each breast.

Keeley felt heat building within her. She was going to leap right off this bed if Prue did one more little thing to her. And then Prue did, gently taking Keeley's hardened nipple between her teeth and tugging on it, just a little. Keeley felt herself start to go.

"No!" She rolled to the side, dumping Prue from her, gasping and struggling to pull the sheet tightly to her body. "I can't do this, Prue. I can't!"

Prue sat up, her shadowed form looking small and vulnerable. Keeley wanted to grab her, hold her closely, protect her forever.

"You seemed ready, Keeley."

Prue sounded terribly sad, and Keeley knew she was crying. She strained to not touch the tearful woman. If she did she'd be in a fearful muddle. "I can't, Prue. I just can't."

"It's Attie, isn't it?"

Keeley looked sharply at Prue's dark form. "Attie? Attie ain't got nothing to do with this."

"Isn't she your sweetheart?"

"No! Attie don't do this stuff."

"And I do. And so do you."

"I guess we do. We just did. Well, we almost did." Keeley put up a protesting hand. "But we stopped. Somebody might think we were crazy if they ever learned about it. I think we are."

Prue flopped backward onto the thick, down pillows. "Oh, Keeley, we're not any such thing. We just like each other and were about to enjoy each other. That's all."

"Well," Keeley drawled, "it ain't enough. A body ought to care about someone a whole lot more than that before they carry on like we were about to."

"And you and Attie don't."

"Absolutely not." Keeley spoke with a staccato voice. "She's a good girl."

"And you've never made love, either. Man or woman."

Keeley paused too long, but it was too late now. She continued lying. "Never."

"Well, then, the town has been wrong about you two all along. And I was too."

Redressed now, Keeley pulled down her gown until it covered her toes. "What's the town wrong about?"

"That you and Attie are sweethearts?"

"That's a lie!" Keeley lay down and angrily yanked the remaining blankets from Prue. "I got to get some sleep, Prue. Good night."

She listened to Prue quietly weeping, aching to hold her, hungering to touch her. She raved silently, wishing Prue meant nothing, that Attie meant nothing. If she had to care for someone, she longed to care for only one person at a time, not two, and not when she already lived with one of them.

She wished she could retract her lies. Even being here with Prue was a lie. She didn't give a damn about the bell. She had come on this trip with the hopes that this very thing would happen. And now look what it had cost her. Money, oh yes, plenty of money — all that she had in the world. And it had cost her her honor. She was a liar and a cheat. That's what a man was called who slept with another woman — not counting the town's saloon ladies. Worse, another woman had put her hands all over places on

Keeley's body that had never been touched by another living soul other than her ma and Attie.

Oh, God, Attie, her heart cried out. *What am I doing here?* Agonizing over the question, and steadfastly refusing to touch Prue, who would not return to her own bed, she fell into a troubled sleep.

The following morning, Prue seemed completely unperturbed by the previous night's tryst. She awoke tossing aside the small corner of blanket that she had managed to wrest from Keeley and threw back the draperies. Robustly, she began singing "Jeanie with the Light Brown Hair." Keeley struggled to peel open her eyes and watched through tiny slits as Prue went into the bathroom. She closed them again, thinking that another night like last night, and she'd be unable to fend off Prue. Maybe she could find an all-night card game somewhere on the train, not that she had money to play, but she could watch until dawn.

Again Keeley paid for Prue's meal, resenting it and resenting that Prue had not made an offer to pick up the tab. And then her anger melted as Prue sipped coffee from a thin china cup while watching Keeley over the steaming brim. "You do have pretty eyes, Prue," Keeley said, setting aside her resentment.

"You are a sweet and wonderful woman, Keeley. I envy whoever will win your heart. You have honor, and you have courage. I wish I could be the one for you."

Keeley wasn't going to talk with Prue about honor and courage, but she did say as she dropped her gaze, "Be strange, two women like that."

"Only if the women themselves believed it to be strange. I wouldn't."

Keeley wondered about that. She wanted to ask

why Prue was so taken with Hawk Blackbean if she was so equally taken with Keeley, but she didn't dare. She was acutely relieved that nothing had happened last night, that she was still true to Attie and that Prue was still a beautiful flower to look at without guilt. Keeley wasn't willing to let go of any of that. "I don't suppose it would be strange, then, Prue. But other folks would think so."

"I just wouldn't tell them." Prue looked so self-possessed, so sure of herself. Keeley's heart swelled with love for her. She was very glad after all that she had decided to come on this trip.

Later, just before departure, a porter entered the parlor car where Keeley and Prue had settled themselves for the start of their return journey. He led a portly bewhiskered man wearing a dark-brown business suit to where they sat. "Pardon me, Miss Morris," he said. "A gentleman to see you." The porter left as the tall man removed his hat and introduced himself.

"Mr. Bacheller at your service, Miss Morris. I understand you are the escort for the Omaha bell."

Prue offered her hand without rising. "I am, indeed, Mr. Bacheller. Won't you be seated?"

"I'm sure you're very busy," he said, sitting gingerly on the edge of a blue velvet chair across from her, "so, I'll be brief. I just need to take possession of your draft, and you'll be on your way. Here is your guarantee of delivery assuring you that everything is in order." Keeley watched him with disinterested eyes.

"Of course," Prue said. She withdrew an envelope from her bag and handed it to him.

"Your guarantee, ma'am."

Accepting the precious document, she said, "Omaha will be very happy."

As he rose to leave, he said with obvious pride, "Your bell has been carefully crated and loaded, Miss Morris. Thirty tons, seventy-seven percent copper and twenty-three percent tin, as promised. It has a beautiful tone, and your townsmen's names are done in excellent, delicate relief. The framework is of oak. The clapper will have to be reattached when the bell is hung, and the headstock is —"

"I'm sure everything is in order, Mr. Bacheller. Pass and Stowe is an excellent forge."

"We cast the Liberty Bell, you know."

"Yes," Prue said impatiently. "I'm aware of the city's history. Thank you." Her eyes abruptly dismissed him.

After he had gone, Keeley said, "He talks a lot."

Prue waved off Keeley's comment with a flick of her hand. "Business is business. He was beginning to bore me." She drifted off, absently gazing out the window.

"How do they make a bell, Prue?" Keeley asked, but Prue seemed deep in thought, so deep that Keeley thought she had better leave her alone with her pondering.

A whistle blew, and Keeley felt the train give a jerk. She listened to a man shout "All aboooard" just outside her car and watched the train slowly pull out of the station and out of the city.

Chapter Eleven

As much as she wanted it to happen, Keeley lay awake every night, fretful that Prue might climb into bed with her again. She need not have concerned herself. With each new morning's arrival, Prue was safely in her own berth while Keeley had needlessly lost another night's sleep.

An enthusiastic brass band of five played "Camptown Races," while at least half of Omaha was on hand to welcome home their bell when the train pulled into the station late the next day.

"I'll help unload that bell. Which car's it in?" a

dozen or so men asked above the cheering cluster of people straining to get a first look at the treasure. A thin, lithe fellow leaped into the first freight car. "Nope, not in this one." As a body they trooped to the next, getting in the handlers' way and generally making nuisances of themselves. The bell wasn't in there, either. "Hey, where's the bell, Prue?" came a shout.

"Look in the last one, Nate!" Again, the crowd moved.

Keeley waited on the platform with Prue while Bill Taylor interviewed her. "This'll be a great story, Miss Webster." He scribbled rapidly on a small notepad with the stub of a pencil. She smiled broadly, looking as if the sun filled her eyes.

Listening to their exchange, Keeley grinned, equally happy, not because the bell had finally reached its destination, but because she was going home in a few minutes. No more noise. No more spending money she didn't have. No more having to be strong when Prue was near her. She'd straighten things out with Attie and never think about the bell or Prue again, and she'd work real hard on the Prue part.

One dray had already been loaded and driven off. A second, with a team of four mules, waited to transport the bell. It would be taken directly to the church, where celebrations arranged by the parish women would begin at noon on Sunday.

"Come on, Nate, look in the last car," an impatient male voice shouted. "And get that damn dray out of the way! Where is it, Miss Prue?" the voice called. "Where's the bell?"

Prue glanced toward the crowd, her attention drawn away from the editor. Her smile never changed as she said, "I'll be right back, Bill. I've got to see what they're yelling about." Keeley tagged along to see what was going on. "What's the problem, John?" Prue asked a rangy cowhand as she reached them. The exuberant band still blew "Camptown Races," and she had to shout to be heard.

"The bell ain't on the train, ma'am," he said. "We all looked."

"Well, then," she replied confidently. "I'll see for myself, because I know it's here, and it's just too big to lose." She mounted the steps to the car and removed from her pocketbook the document that Mr. Bacheller had given her before they'd left Philadelphia. She held it aloft like a banner of surrender. "Look, here's our bill of sale and guarantee of delivery." She was assisted in and out of the cars, looking inside each. Her task completed, she stood at the edge of the final car. "There's been some kind of a mistake," she declared. She held her head high and her shoulders square. "I was told that it was loaded three mornings ago." Her eyes glazed slightly, replaced by a tinge of fear.

Keeley was terribly disappointed that the bell wasn't on the train, not for herself but for Prue, who had worked so hard so that Omaha could have something it was proud of and could talk about for years to come. Prue loved Omaha, and that was the truth of it.

Attempting to sound confident once again, Prue declared, "We'll send a telegram or two and find out where our bell is."

"I'll do it," Hawk Blackbean pronounced from the outer ring of the group. Clean-shaven, he wore no hat and his clothing, a blue cotton shirt and blue pants, was tidy. His hair was neatly trimmed. He looked at Prue across the heads of the others with something akin to ownership showing in his eyes. Keeley felt her stomach tighten.

Prue shaded her eyes against the lowering sun. "Thank you, Mr. Blackbean." Relief filled her voice. Keeley wondered why Prue had such confidence in the rascal. "Pass Mr. Blackbean the guarantee, would you, John?" she asked, handing it to him. "The address is on it." John hesitated before surrendering the document. It traveled quietly from hand to hand until it made its way to where Hawk waited.

Keeley cursed under her breath. She should have thought right off to send a telegram. Anybody should have spoken up before Hawk did.

Hawk held up the paper, showing Prue that it had reached him, then went into the station to send a telegram.

"We'll wait," Prue said, stepping down from the car. The baggage handler assisted her to the walkway. The crowd had thinned considerably. They would return when the bell was on the train for sure.

"Well, he came along just in time, didn't he?" Prue said to Keeley.

"Just in time," she said flatly.

Bill Taylor joined them. "I'll stop over to your restaurant later, Miss Morris, and see what happened. People will want to follow this story closely." Keeley smirked inwardly, envisioning Wednesday's *Omaha's* headline: WHERE IS OMAHA'S SIXTY-THOUSAND-POUND BELL? Likely, it was on the next scheduled train due in two days from now, not much excitement in predictability, though. Taylor smiled, tipped his hat and left.

The few who remained milled around, waiting for Blackbean to bring them some news. Little more than an hour passed before he came out of the station and pronounced, "There ain't no bell coming here to Omaha. It never got shipped to us."

After the silence came the loud question, "Where, then?"

"Nobody seems to know," Blackbean answered. "I got two telegrams here that says the same thing. One from Stove and Pass Forge that made the bell and one from the Northern Pacific Railway yardmaster who makes sure things gets to where they're going. They both say that according to the paperwork, it made it onto the train. *This* train. They're dead sure. Well, it ain't here, gentlemen."

"What about other trains or the freight cars sittin' in the yard?" Nate asked.

"Telegram here says they checked. That's probably what took them so long to reply. Here, read it for yourselves." But no one reached for the notes.

The silence grew until someone asked, "But what about our money? We're talkin' four thousand dollars here. What about that?" They had all worked hard. Even the children had pitched in by making cookies and selling them door to door, then delivering their change to Prue. Every citizen had waited a long time for this moment that was supposed to have been a wonderful and wild celebration. Their faces turned toward Prue.

"I don't know what happened," she said. She gazed off toward the horizon, allowing several seconds to pass before continuing. "We'll find our bell, ladies and gentlemen, and you children too." She rested her hand against the cheek of a small girl standing beside her.

"It's ours, and we'll bring that bell home. I promise."
She picked up her bag and walked away from them,
passing through the gathering with her head still held
high. She wasn't going to stand for something like
this to happen to Omaha, and Keeley wasn't going to
let it happen to Prue. Likely no one else in town
would, either.

Prue's voice became low and shaking as Keeley
grabbed her bag and walked with her toward the
restaurant. "It was on this train, Keeley," she said. "I
know it was. Why would anybody want to steal a bell?
You can't even make bullet casings from it." She
stopped suddenly and walked the short distance back
to the station where people still mingled. "All right,
then," she said lightly. "You can't very well just walk
off with a sixty-thousand-pound bell, now, can you?
I'm inviting you all over to my place, and I'll make
sure everybody has a good cup of coffee just for
greeting me like you did." She signaled toward the
musicians. "And bring the band along too. Thank you,
ladies and gentlemen. Thank you all very much." They
cheered her as they followed behind.

Keeley didn't move. "I'll see you later, Prue. Looks
like you've got your hands full."

"Thank you for going with me, Keeley. Thank you
for everything. You don't know how helpful you've
been. It's been wonderful."

Keeley fought a rising heartbeat as Prue kissed her
lightly on the cheek before going on. Hawk Blackbean
moved in alongside her and took her luggage.

"Well, Jingles," Keeley said to the horse she had
yet to retrieve. "I know you'll be glad to see me even
if everybody else has already forgot that I was on that
trip too — if they even knew."

Stars were beginning to twinkle in the clear, late-evening sky. Keeley loped toward home with a fearful steel band wrapped tight around her chest. Would Attie be there when she arrived? The band drew tighter as she neared the soddy. No light shone through the window. If Attie had left her, then Keeley was a doomed soul. In case she was wrong and Attie was in bed, Keeley would first take care of Jingles; then, when she crawled beside her, she'd be able to take Attie in her arms without interruption and hold her all night long. How glad she was that she was home where she belonged, not someplace in some city chasing after feelings she had no right having.

She turned Jingles into the pasture and headed for the soddy. As soon as she opened the door, she had her answer. Attie was gone. Inside, it was cold enough to know that there hadn't been a fire in the stove for several days.

She left her bag by the door. In the dark, she kicked off her boots, dropped her clothes at her feet and fell nude onto the bed. She pulled the covers over her chest and rested an arm across her forehead while she stared into the night. Out of habit she brushed her foot across the bottom of the mattress, as she did every night, checking for the Mason jar Attie had brought with her when she moved in. It was gone, of course. She was sure that Attie had left Keeley's share of the money on the table. She knew where Attie was. She rolled her head toward the direction of Attie's house where they had first met. Those were good days. Good, good days.

Keeley tossed and turned until dawn, unable to recall a worse night since burying the last of her family. Once more, she was alone. She passionately longed to relive her life from the moment she had first said to Prue, "How about if I go to Philadelphia with you? I could be good company and make sure that the bell gets back here too." She hadn't been good company. She'd felt wretched most of the trip, fiercely wanting Prue and at the same time not wanting her while she spent most of the trip just staring out windows and later, not even remembering what she'd seen. There had been strong feelings of guilt because of Attie, and all the lying she'd done. And now the bell loomed big again. There would be an all-out search for the thing. Well, to hell with finding it! How was she going to get her Attie back?

A few days later she made her biweekly trip to Omaha. She was more interested in the most recent news than she was in replenishing her flour and bacon. Likely, the creation had turned up by now. As she entered Prue's restaurant, she found her seated at a table and surrounded by a small knot of men. Keeley quietly greeted them as she removed her hat and joined Prue.

"Morning, Prue, and you too, Delaney." Hawk Blackbean had come in right behind Keeley.

Keeley nodded as Blackbean hung his hat on the back of a chair. His manners were surely improving. Like yesterday, he wore a cotton shirt, red today, and blue jeans instead of his usual greasy leather garb. He looked — handsome. Hawk was sparking Prue. Keeley knew it!

The talk quieted as Prue repeated for those who had just come in, "I found this pinned to my door this morning when I opened up. Someone knows where the bell is." She lay a small rumpled sheet in the middle of the table. The note was soiled with fingerprints and crumpled as though it had been carried in a pocket for a while.

Keeley picked it up and read: *I hve scrapd of 1 name. Messerschmit. 1000 dolrs or anotr name gos. 5000 dolrs 4 the bel.*

"I just don't understand how anyone could do this. It's so vicious and cruel. I've sent telegram after telegram to the foundry to see what is going on. All I receive back is bad news. And now this!" Prue broke into sobs as Keeley returned the message.

Hawk moved through the circle and squatted beside Prue. His black eyes were set; his jaw muscles bulged outward as he clenched his teeth. "We'll get the bell for you, Prue. We'll bring it back and hang it in the church. And then it'll ring for the children and services and weddings, just like you talked about."

Weddings? Prue talked to Blackbean about weddings? Keeley wanted to leave. She was about to do that when Prue asked, "What do you think, Keeley?"

Who cared what she thought? She didn't have any say in this. Hawk's look told her that, and so did a number of the rest of the men. "About what?"

"Look at this note. It's terrible!"

Keeley glanced again at the paper lying ominous and threatening on the tabletop. "I'd like to know more about what it means."

Blackbean snatched it up. "It means, Delaney, that we pay a thousand dollars to keep anybody else's name from being scraped off. And we pay five thousand to get the bell back."

126

"Which means," a stocky man said, "that it's going to be cheaper to pay the six grand right away than to pay one thousand for each name they destroy if we delay and don't give them the money right now."

"Pay the six grand, then," Jack Toner, the Bar E owner, said quickly.

"Yeah? How?" came the immediate and surly question from the counter where farmer Noot Smith had been listening.

"Well, we managed to raise enough for the bell," Alan Boody, another rancher, and a very wealthy one, pointed out.

Barker Tabbet spoke angrily, his thick, dark brows rising and falling with each word. "Easy for you to say, Boody. My wife worked for weeks on benefits and darned near baked me out of house and home. I ain't paying another six thousand for no bell that ought to be hanging in a new-built church belfry right now. Or a thousand, neither."

"Your name's on it, Tabbet. Don't you care about that?" Blackbean asked.

"Not as much as I care about my money, I don't."

Blackbean rose, stretching to his full six feet, three inches. "Well, by God, I do," he said. He looked each man in the eye. "My name's on there, and it means something to me. The Blackbeans mean something around here, they do."

A good number of eyes quickly shifted, looking at walls, the ceiling, their boots. Keeley knew what they were thinking, and so was she: an occasional missing cow from somebody's herd, a guaranteed drunken brawl every Friday and Saturday night, an occasional knifing with Blackbean always suspect and getting off scot-free.

"It can't be that hard," he was saying, "to find a big bell like that." He looked straight at Keeley. "You did a fine job getting it back here, Delaney. You better stay home this time and cook or something. That'd suit you better."

"Hawk!" Prue scolded.

"Never mind, Prue," Keeley said quietly. One day Hawk Blackbean would get his comeuppance.

Again, giving his attention to Prue, he said, "I'll find that bell, Miss Prue, and I'll bring it to you myself, and I'll bet ten dollars that Messerschmit goes too. It was his family's name they took off." He rammed on his hat and headed for the door.

"How do you know they took off Messerschmit's name, Blackbean?" Boody asked sharply. "Just because this note says so? Maybe it ain't so."

Prue burst into renewed tears. She raised her hands, saying, "Please, please, gentlemen."

Hawk didn't answer, and soon the door's bells stopped jangling.

Oh, how Keeley wanted to find the bell and proudly deliver it to Prue herself before that miserable Blackbean did.

And she still had to straighten out her and Attie's problem too. If she had been feeling good when she rode in this morning, it was all gone now. She might as well have been carrying around an ox yoke on her shoulders so hard did her troubles weight her down.

Chapter Twelve

Sheriff Butts and Hawk Blackbean, the only two men who ended up tracking the bell, returned empty-handed two weeks later. By train and carriage and at the expense of Omaha's taxpayers, they had followed the trail from the Philadelphia foundry to the train station, to the loading dock and to the correct freight car. They sent telegrams and searched the freight yards and made a nuisance of themselves at the forge. Then they returned to Omaha with their tails between their legs. Butts telegraphed ahead with the news of the unsuccessful trip and the time of their expected return. Prue sent word to Keeley asking that she be at the restaurant when Butts showed up. It gladdened Keeley's heart that Prue hadn't mentioned Hawk at all.

She was occupying a stool at the counter when the doorbell rang and Blackbean entered. He removed his hat and raked his fingers through his disheveled hair. A few customers sat around smoking and drinking coffee. Prue set down the coffeepot and came around the counter to greet him.

"Butts went to his office," Hawk said, stopping before Prue and looking down on her with sadness deep in his voice. "He'll be over later." He looked weary and contrite. Keeley took a great deal of satisfaction from that.

Even having been told ahead of time that the men hadn't located the bell, Prue, looking haggard and worried herself, had still held out hope. She rested her slender hands on his arms. "You tried," she said simply.

He removed his hat, looking much like his old self after his long journey. His buckskins were greasy and saddle worn, his hair uncombed, and he badly needed a shave. Keeley found his old, familiar bedraggled appearance strangely comforting. "There wasn't a sign, Prue," he said in his low, rumbling voice. "It's like the thing never existed. The forge says they shipped it. The railroad says they loaded it. Their papers are in order."

"Then there's nothing? Nothing at all?" Prue asked. Keeley gritted her teeth as she watched Prue's hands tighten on Blackbean's arms.

Hawk's eyes never wavered as he said, "I'm sorry, Prue."

She sank to a nearby chair and leaned her elbows on the table. She took a deep breath and paused before saying, "There've been a few more notes from the bell thief. He sticks them up all over the place, on stores, a couple on the newspaper office. Most have been pinned to my back door. A few on the front. Your name's been eliminated from the bell. So have the Delaneys and the Joneses. Seven altogether now."

"My God, Prue," Hawk said as he joined her at the table. "We can't pay that. It's more than the ransom is." Keeley stepped close to Prue's side as Hawk's expression shifted from looking tired and sad to one of anger and vindication. A vein in his forehead swelled and pulsed like a thick, black snake; little fires grew in his eyes.

"Here." Prue withdrew several scraps of paper from her apron pocket. "I call them notes of pure gall. Whoever is doing this is obviously having a wonderful time at Omaha's expense."

Hawk leafed through them. "Does he leave notes every day?"

"Night, and not every night. Did you see the one there that says if we don't pay, the bell is going to be completely destroyed? Although I don't know how you could completely destroy a thirty-ton bell."

"Probably roll it off a cliff somewhere," Hawk suggested wearily. He flopped his hat on the table and leaned back in his chair.

"Then let him destroy it," Keeley declared, joining them. Those at the counter watched but remained quiet. Even Timmy had stopped serving. "It'd be cheaper just to order up a new bell."

Hawk stood, staring down at her with icy, coal-black eyes. She glared right back, but felt her insides grow weak beneath his bullying scowl. He said, "I designed that bell, Delaney. Miss Prue raised the money for it, and she collected up all the names to put on it." Keeley could smell days' old breath and tobacco odors wafting from his mouth. Short, individual whiskers grew dark from his face, and his wiry eyebrows protruded helter-skelter. There were streaks of gray throughout his hair she'd never seen before. His demeanor made her quake, but she held herself firm while he continued speaking in a low monotone designed, she was sure, to frighten her. It did. "It ain't a new bell we need here, Keeley. It's the bell that Prue worked so hard for that we need, and we're gonna get it back."

It was impossible for Keeley to peel her gaze from his face. She couldn't afford to. He would know how he terrorized her. She listened to feet shuffling in the silence of the room. Apparently, someone at the counter had risen from his stool. Another cleared his throat. Hawk's riveting look shifted, releasing her. She didn't dare move a muscle, possibly catching his attention again, but she thought she looked brave through it all.

"Hawk," thin Jason Farley said, "maybe Keeley's got something, there. You could design the bell again. You still got the plans?"

"It ain't the same, Jason," Hawk said forcefully. "It'd be a different bell. We can carve the missing names back on with a knife or something. You men want to let some thief do this to you? Your wives and kids worked hard for that bell, and you donated plenty of money to buy it." His hand swung wide, encompassing their silent gazes. "Now, you tell me you'd just as soon buy another bell and forget what's been done

132

to us." He stalked to the door, the heels of his boots striking sharply against the floor. "Well, not me, boys. I'm gonna get Miss Prue that bell back. And I ain't paying one red cent to do it, either. I'm gonna catch the man that stole it, and then I'm gonna shoot him." He stopped with his hand on the doorknob. "I'm gonna bring you your bell, Prue, and I'll put the names back on it for you and hang it too. And to hell with the rest of you for giving up so easy." He stared them all down one at a time, then quietly let himself out.

Keeley and the rest released a single collective breath. The sound would have been comical except for the knot in her gut.

"That man can scare me so at times," Prue said.

"What do you think, Miss Prue?" Abel Kent asked. Everlastingly dressed in black, he was the town's dentist, doctor and undertaker.

Prue's shoulders slumped. "I just don't know, Dr. Kent." Keeley watched Prue's hands shaking as they rested in her lap. She wanted to hold them, steady them, pass her strength to them. "I suppose we could just reorder, but we worked so hard for this one . . ." Her voice trailed off, taken over by quiet sobs as her entire being began to tremble.

John North, a tall, heavy man whose ranch lay several miles outside of Omaha, spoke up. "Let's go home, boys, and let Miss Prue alone. She's had enough. There's a Cattlemen's Association meeting Monday night at the church. We can talk about what to do then."

"And what if Blackbean insists on not buying a new bell and just forgets the ransom?" a second rancher asked.

"For once, Blackbean's right," Tod North, the son of John North, replied. He was growing into a big man and one as tough and honest as his hardworking father and just a little hotter under the collar than his old man had once been. "There ain't gonna be no ransoms, and there ain't gonna be a new bell. We're going to get this one back. It belongs to Omaha, and it's gonna hang in our church and school just where it's supposed to. The only difference is that Blackbean ain't gonna hang it up there by hisself. And I'll shoot him down like a dog if I have to to be a part of putting it up there."

It was an oath. Some muttered their assent. Others shook their heads in disagreement. It was Prue's dream, her creation, her wonderful gift to Omaha.

Keeley bid Prue a brief good-bye. Throwing her leg across Jingles, she neverj once thought that she was again deeply involving herself in Prue's affairs and emotions, not recognizing that her own longings for Prue were again rampant. She accepted her sentiments blindly, thinking as she rode from town that she'd go get that Attie woman on the way home too.

By damn, she was going to have it all.

Chapter Thirteen

A weird November thunderstorm was blowing in from the west bringing with it steady, cold rain and hail the size of tiny stones that fell from dense, black clouds hanging thick and low over the land.

In spite of her large hat and a long rainproof duster worn over her sheepskin jacket, Keeley still rode soaked to the skin, shivering and hunched in the saddle and longing to kick the stuffing out of Jingles. The weather was making him feisty as she rode the fence line, and he wouldn't behave, stubbornly moving at his own plodding pace. She pulled her coat tighter and hat lower, but it did little good as chilling water dribbled down her neck and over her spine. Her gloves were soaked, and her hands ached within the slimy leather as the reins hung limp between her fingers.

She was sick at heart and considering just falling from the saddle, lying in the mud and letting the increasingly hard downpour beat her and Jingles to death. And of course, the bell was missing. And that little restaurant owner just wouldn't leave her mind alone. But that wasn't the worst of it. That happened yesterday after Blackbean had scared her so badly in Prue's restaurant.

Leaving the Prudence Jane Restaurant, she had felt downright full of pine-pitch and vinegar from having at least looked like she'd stood up to Hawk and completely confident that Attie would come home with her that day. All she had to do was go get her. What she was greeted with was a switch-wielding, irrational, angry woman telling her to get back to her soddy and stay there. That knocked her right out of the saddle, so to speak.

"Have you gone crazy, Attie?" Keeley shouted as she yanked Jingles away from the whip that struck the horse instead of her, Attie's intended victim. "You been living alone too long. You lost your mind, woman."

"Found it, Keeley. Now, go on home, and leave me alone."

Keeley went to Attie's twice more that week with the same results. Attie grabbed a switch and came after her.

"It's that Prue woman, Jingles," she said to the plodding gelding. "I gotta forget her once and for all. Just like I did before." She fell silent as more miles slid beneath her mount's hooves. After much thought, she continued, "I'm gonna get my Attie back, old horse, if it takes forever. She means too much to me." But did she mean more than Prue and her bell? Attie was going to have to understand that Keeley still needed to find the bell the same as everybody else in town wanted to do, but only because they had all worked so hard for it. "And for no other reason, Jingles," she added without believing it.

She pictured some demented, scraggly, no-account individual hovering over Omaha's bell, a file in his clawlike hands, destroying names one by one as he cackled like a madman. The more she thought about it, the angrier she became. She cursed the thief, the weather and her heart that was constantly being torn in two as she waffled between her feelings for Attie and Prue. She cursed the whole world and all the people in it. She pulled Jingles up so short, he reared and slipped in the mud, throwing her sideways in the saddle. When he landed, she leaped from his back. Mud splayed from beneath her boots, and her raincoat flew around her legs. She tore her hat from her head and turned her face upward where rain and hail fell upon her exposed skin. She screamed her outrage into the storm as her arms flailed in the air, and her bootheels gouged the earth. She stamped about uncontrollably as Jingles tossed his head and rolled his eyes and moved away from her.

Sobbing, she found herself on her hands and knees with mud oozing between the fingers of her gloves and heavy drops of rain and ice still battering her body. She squatted on her haunches, waiting for her sobs to subside. When that happened, she mounted up, thinking she might again try to see Attie.

She reached home an hour later. It was nearly dark, and she hurried to stable Jingles before the light was completely gone. In the soddy, she hung her outerwear on a nearby peg. She got a good fire going, heated up water in the cauldron and took a standing bath. Wrapped in a clean flannel shirt, wool socks and denim pants, she crawled into bed. She was asleep in less than five minutes, effectively blocking out her fear of losing Attie forever and the argument she knew would ensue when she revealed that she was going to look for the bell and its thief.

Remarkably, Attie agreed to talk with her the following morning as Keeley stood outside the door, and Attie lingered inside with her hand on the handle. Maybe it was the pleasantly warm day and clear sky with not a cloud marring its silvery-blue surface that had softened Attie's heart. Keeley didn't care what it was. She was just grateful that Attie wasn't flailing that switch at her.

"Who cares what you do, Keeley?" Attie said sharply. "Go right ahead and look for the bell. You'd rather do that than go after your horses and tend to your own knitting, anyway. Why do you think I left you? Because you've got a big heart? Because you care about the damn bell? No! It's because you don't have a brain in your head, and you can't make up your mind." She was furious, her eyes blazing as she shook a finger at Keeley. She wore her hair piled high on her head, and it glistened in the sunlight. Keeley reached out to touch the shining tresses. Attie viciously slapped her hand aside. "Not on your life,

Keeley Delaney. You and your damn bell. And that Prue woman too."

Keeley's anger surfaced. "You're just mad because you didn't go to Philadelphia too."

Attie's jaw dropped along with her voice. "That's what you think this is about, Keeley? Some stupid trip? My God!" Shaking her head, she slowly closed the door in Keeley's face.

Attie's reaction paralyzed Keeley. Recovering herself, she pounded on the door, yelling, "Open this door, Attie Webster," but it remained closed. "Come on, Attie," Keeley pleaded. "You know it ain't about the bell. It's about you coming on home."

From inside came the bitter retort, "I am home. You go on home, yourself. Go find your old bell. Go find somebody else that'll do for you what I did for the past two years."

"All right, then, I will," Keeley muttered to herself. She turned away. Attie wouldn't have her. At least that part was settled. That left the bell. She'd have to find the thing soon. Or someone would. Omaha was turning angry. It seemed like the whole place was going to hell over one damn bell. Luckily, there was still Prue, the one remaining light in Keeley's life. Prue would live with her if Attie wouldn't and maybe even tend the garden. Keeley would ask her at the first opportunity. The idea didn't set entirely true, but she foolishly and stubbornly ignored her misgivings.

For the next few days, she tediously labored at straightening the soddy, which had become a jumble of dishes, clothing and tools, and working on the barn, shoring up the plank walls. Jingles busied himself with rolling around on his back in the now-dead grass and dirt and nipping and kicking at the other horses

139

as he asserted his place in the herd. Keeley was restless and warranted that Jingles was too.

Within the week, she returned to the prairie on the off-chance she could shag a horse or two before winter hit the prairies full blast. This time, when she had a good bunch of horses ready to sell, she'd pay a man to do her trading for her. It had been a costly lesson, discovering that it wasn't sound business sense trying to sell the herd as a woman.

In a few days' time, she managed to bring home three feisty mares, grateful all the way to the bottoms of her boots that the snows hadn't yet come. She turned the horses out to pasture, and the following morning, after a solid night's sleep, rode into Omaha.

She felt good about her successful catch in only a short amount of time, though Attie constantly remained in her ever-conflicting thoughts. It exasperated her that Attie and Prue, so different from each other, battled for her unsettled heart.

Riding directly to Prue's restaurant, she slipped from the saddle and tossed the reins over the rail. At the counter, several men were devouring huge breakfasts.

"Morning, Timmy. Coffee." Prue wasn't there. Timmy nodded and poured her a mug, then slid the sugar and a small pitcher of milk over to her as she settled on a stool. She bypassed them, asking, "Prue around?" Her heard pounded in anticipation. She could barely wait to see Prue again. Things were going to be different between them. If Prue wanted to kiss her, then Keeley was going to let her.

"She's over at the church."

"What for?"

Timmy grinned his big, toothy smile. "Big doings

Saturday night. She's right there in the thick of it, you know."

Of course Prue would be. Keeley never knew anybody who socialized the way that woman did. It would be a problem if Prue kept it up after they were together. Keeley lived a good hour from Omaha. Besides that, she didn't go in for much socializing, although lately she couldn't say that. "What's going on?" she asked.

"Gonna be a big dance this Saturday night. Miss Prue's raising money for the bell."

"For ransom money?"

"Either that or to buy a new bell again. Guess the town wants to be sure to have money, in case they can't catch the bell thief after all."

Keeley swallowed the last of her scalding coffee. "We'll catch him, Timmy. Then we'll hang him." She paid up and rode over to the church.

Keeley looked around as she entered. The pews had been pushed against the walls. Oaken buckets stuffed with late-season wildflowers decorated the room's corners and the altar. The teacher's desk and two nearby tables were already burdened with a variety of baked goods.

"Morning, Prue." Keeley's boot-steps echoed hollowly within the high-ceilinged building.

"Keeley!" Prue rushed over from the desk where she had been giving some flowers a last-minute touch-up. "Where've you been? So much has happened." Keeley reached to wrap Prue in her arms and hold her there forever, but Prue was in and out of her grasp before Keeley knew what had happened. This wasn't the greeting she'd expected. But then, they were inside a church and school.

Keeley tossed her hat onto a pew. "I stopped at the restaurant. Timmy said there's going to be a dance."

"That's right." Although she looked drawn and tired and perhaps a bit thinner, Prue's eyes were bright and glowing. "The town's decided to go ahead and try to raise as much money as possible. We've put an advertisement in the newspaper hoping to draw people in."

"What good will that do? The paper only gets read right here in town."

"Bill Taylor said he's going to print extra copies and send them to Sioux City, Fremont, Bellevue and of course, to the fort. I'm sure lots of soldiers will want to come." She had returned to the desk and was rearranging the baked goods. "You'll be here, won't you?"

Keeley scoffed. "Not a chance."

"Oh, come on, Keeley. Be a friend."

"I wouldn't fit in."

"Sure you would. Wear a dress. Just this once, Keeley." Prue turned pleading eyes upon her. "Please. You don't have to dance. You could help me sell food and punch."

Keeley cringed and felt her skin crawl at the thought of a skirt dangling around her legs. Yet she said, "Just this once."

"And bring a basket of food. We're going to auction off box lunches. That should bring in some money too."

"The soldiers will kill each other and spend every dime they have. Not that many girls around here."

Prue smiled wickedly. "Exactly."

That Saturday, Keeley drove to town using her

own rickety wagon, Attie having taken hers with her when she left. She wore the only dress she owned. It still fit and was still pretty. Her mother had been a fine seamstress, insisting that Pa and Aaron have at least one fine linen shirt and one good suit and that Keeley have a pretty green dress, gathered at the waist and tied tightly with a bow. Keeley hated it, but she imagined she did look attractive in it even after all these years. She rammed her feet into a pair of low-cut, black leather shoes that buttoned to the ankle, and then brushed her hair until it shone before tying it back with a green ribbon. As uncomfortable as she felt, she thought she could bear it for one evening.

The dance began at five. Keeley would have been willing to bet that with the shorter days upon them, the ranchmen and farmers were grumbling for having to quit work so early for a dance.

By the time she arrived, wagons and buggies were parked everywhere. Lantern light beamed from every window of the church From inside, men's heavy laughter and women's high giggles mixed pleasantly with rowdy fiddle music, strong fingers beating out an accompanying rhythm against some woman's ribbed washboard and the wailing of a mouth organ. The sounds of feet stamped along to the beat. Children, screaming with laughter, raced in and out of the door and chased one another around the building, ducking beneath vehicles and horses' and mules' bellies. She supposed she ought to tell them not to do that, but they wouldn't have listened to her. She wouldn't have if she were their age. This was a night for fun, and that meant everybody.

Dismounting, her heavy coat snagged between the

brake-stick and the seat. She yanked at the thick, wool cloth, cursing beneath her breath as she impatiently righted her dress.

Overbearing heat struck her as she stepped inside the crammed building. The place reverberated with gyrating bodies dancing at a fast pace to the merry music. Regulars, out-of-towners and dozens of soldiers were there, proving that Prue's idea of having Bill Taylor send his paper farther afield was a wise move. She was suddenly glad that she had agreed to wear her dress. Every woman and girl was deckd in her prettiest outfit. There were reds, greens, blues, bright yellows and mixtures of all the colors Keeley could think of. The gentlemen's dark coats and pants were pressed and their boots wiped clean of mud. Beards and moustaches had been trimmed, and if a man had neither, his face was scrubbed to a shine. Soldiers wore pressed uniforms with buttons shining and boots gleaming. They stood ramrod straight, their hats tucked beneath their arms as they waited for an opportunity to dance. Everyone looked nice and, she thought with pride, so did she.

"May I take your things, Miss Keeley?" Hosting the door, Timmy greeted her with a smile. He beamed through a freshly shaven face, and his hair was neatly plastered against his forehead. He wore a pressed black suit, white shirt and black string tie. His black boots gleamed.

"My, you look fetching, Timmy," she said, handing him her basket and coat.

His cheeks turned pink as he grinned again and scuffed a boot against the floor like a small lad might do. A young woman Keeley didn't recognize stood by his side smiling adoringly at him.

She shouldered her way through the dancers to the front of the room where pastries and punch were being sold. People waited three and four deep to buy something. The sweets were more elaborately decorated than they had been at the final few sales. Once more, the women were willing to put their hands to the task.

Most people didn't recognize Keeley until she looked directly into their eyes. A number of women's faces registered outright shock, and a greater number of men's jaws dropped. Even Hawk Blackbean was impressed in a backhanded way.

"By golly, you do look pretty, Keeley. How'd you get the dirt off? A wire brush?" He haw-hawed loudly as those standing nearby who overheard his abrasive comment joined tentatively in his laughter. Wives glanced their way, and most of the laughing ceased. Keeley ignored the whole thing. She couldn't very well brain Hawk when she was wearing a dress.

Prue, in a fine gray wool skirt and pale yellow blouse, came from around the table. She gave Hawk a nasty look and gently but possessively drew Keeley away from her tormentors. Depositing her safely behind the tables, she said, "Ignore those men. They're all barbarians."

"They're what?"

Prue didn't answer, and Keeley forgot to ask again as she continued to delight in Prue's warm attention. Prue's hair hung loosely around her shoulders. She had curled it, the waves reminding Keeley of undulating prairie grass on a gentle, windy day.

"You look very, very lovely, Keeley," Prue whispered. She smiled, giving Keeley's arm an affectionate squeeze. Keeley looked doubtful. "It's true,

Keeley. You're actually quite beautiful, my dear friend. Come, pitch right in."

Keeley spent the rest of the evening selling food while Prue flitted here and there making sure things ran smoothly and occasionally taking the time to dance. What made Keeley's blood boil was that she danced most often with Hawk Blackbean.

At evening's end, nothing but empty containers remained; extra tables were carted off by their owners; several men lent a hand returning pews to their proper places; ladies scurried about tidying up while children took turns with the broom. In twenty minutes, the church was back to normal. In another fifteen, only Keeley, Hawk and Prue remained.

"Let's count the money, Miss Prue," Hawk suggested.

"Why's he want to count the money, Prue? What do you need him around for?" Keeley managed to whisper to Prue as Hawk put the final touches on the altar.

"Protection. He's going to walk me back to my place afterward."

Unable to keep the anger from her voice, Keeley snapped, "I can do that. You don't need him."

"Oh, look at you, Keeley. You look like a woman."

"Of course I look like a woman. I *am* a woman. I ain't never denied that. And I'm in a dress!"

"That's just the point. I'm not taking a chance on losing this money."

"I can shoot as well as Hawk Blackbean any day of the week."

"Do you have your gun with you?"

"Not tonight, I don't. Why in hell would I need one tonight?"

"Don't you curse at me, Keeley Delaney. And not here in the Lord's house."

"Now, Prue, you know the men have been drinking and cussing all evening in here, so you got no call to —"

Prue straightened, freezing the rest of Keeley's words in her throat with a frosty-eyed look. "Hawk Blackbean is walking me home after we count the money. You may come with us or not. I need his protection. He's offered, and I've accepted."

"You could have asked me the other day when I was here."

"I could have, Keeley. But I didn't. Now empty the money box, and let's count it."

Keeley boiled with fury, forcing her trembling hands to still themselves as she, Prue and Hawk gathered around the desk to tally the cash.

"Not bad," Hawk said. "There's near four hundred dollars here."

"We should hold another dance right away," Prue suggested. "The soldiers made the difference. They spent the most money."

Hawk's brows creased with thought. "Taylor could send the *Omaha* out even farther next time."

"Good idea," Keeley grudgingly agreed, adding, "Maybe ask for donations too."

"From who?" Hawk asked.

"Businessmen, ranchers, farmers."

"Forget the farmers," Prue said. "Let's see if we can get a couple of ranchers to donate one head each of their cattle. We can auction off the animals. I don't care if we get a dollar for them. It'll be a dollar more."

* * * * *

In the end, they did all that. Omaha became known as the place to go for a good time. As long as the weather was decent that day, there was a dance every Saturday night for the next two months. The saloons were less busy between five and ten at that time, but the owners generously agreed to tolerate the lost revenue. Word spread and donations filtered in. While all this went on, the notes from the bell thief slowed, leading some to believe that he had given up on the ransom and the whole idea of destroying the bell. Others thought he was biding his time, aware that the town was trying its best to raise the entire twelve thousand dollars.

To Keeley, it meant that someone with close connections right here in Omaha knew everything that was going on. Others easily drew the same conclusion and, realizing this, the area's citizens began to look upon one another with suspicion. Additionally, many men had taken up wearing sidearms again, something they hadn't done for a couple of years now that Omaha had settled down into a real legitimate town.

Chapter Fourteen

While the dances continued, Keeley rode to Attie's every three days or so. If nothing else, Attie was still her friend. Keeley never talked to her, nor did she even try to knock on the door. She merely stayed in the saddle near the edge of the woods and stared toward Attie's house. Sometimes Attie would be out hanging clothes or feeding the chickens. Sometimes her wagon would be gone, indicating that she was out gathering and delivering laundry. It was clear from the continuously laden clotheslines that Attie hadn't wasted any time restarting her business. Since she had given up laundering, folks never had had a consistent laundress. Keeley was sure they were glad to see her back on the job again. She had heard around town that Attie was telling people that she missed her own place too much and just went on home. That's what Keeley was telling anyone who asked.

During those times Keeley didn't spot Attie but knew she was somewhere nearby, Keeley's longing to speak to her would become so strong that she needed to bite the reins she held to keep from crying out. Tears poured down her cheeks, and her knuckles whitened as she gripped the saddle horn. When she could bear no more pain, she rode away and dragged herself through her work for the rest of the day. She wondered why she tortured herself so but could think of no way to stop or even a reason to, and so in a couple of days, she'd again ride over to Attie's, endure the same amount of searing pain and shoulder the increasingly heavy burden of guilt for having lied and for having gone to Philadelphia. Occasionally, she saw Attie driving through Omaha. Keeley held herself together long enough to disappear from town as soon as possible before crying all the way home.

Meanwhile, she carried on, only reluctantly agreeing to help Prue with the dances. Private donations began to filter in from outlying cities. The *Omaha Penny Press* was now printed on a weekly basis instead of its usual single monthly run. Taylor filled his stories with details regarding the bell thief, what he looked like and how he had stolen, maimed and hidden the bell. It was all speculation, of course, because nobody really knew. And the money in the local bank continued to grow.

Weekly, Prue had Taylor print the exact amount of

money the bank held for the bell, and, for a while, the bell thief had been silent. Now the notes had started again.

The day was dark but no snow fell. Keeley was glad that Prue didn't skimp on fuel, keeping the lamp wicks turned up in the table lanterns and along the walls. At a table where she and Prue sat with doughnuts and coffee, she read the bell thief's most recent message: *Yu gut 12,000 dalrs now.*

Tears threatened to spill from Prue's eyes. "Look on the back. There's more."

Keeley read: *I want 3000 more and I will go away.* "*Damn* him!" she shouted. "He's worse than a bank thief. We can't do it!"

The small establishment was quiet during midafternoon. Timmy polished glasses and dusted the thick glass cookie jars on the counter. It would liven up within a couple of hours. Shopkeepers and clerks would be locking up and stopping by for a bite before going home. Over the past several months, more and more women were dropping in, unescorted and confident after closing their own shops for the day.

As time went by, Prue's business had increased, much of the traffic generated by those wanting to hear the latest news regarding Omaha's big, bronze bell, always spoken of in reverent tones.

Over the door outside, Prue had tacked a large white cloth banner with bold black letters announcing, OMAHA'S BELL WILL RETURN. To Keeley, the bell was still just a bell, but the Omahans' once-concerned attitude had changed to that of an obsession, and the more money they'd gathered for the artifact's safe return, the more they'd moved from collectively saying "Our bell" to individually screaming "My bell!" Keeley

151

wanted nothing but to find the damn thing, hang it up and be done with it.

"More money. And then more. And more. It's gotta stop, Prue. How bad do you want this particular bell?"

"I asked everybody that. Everybody! For a while there, they were willing to replace it, but now they say they want only this one. I don't know why in heaven's name they changed their minds." Prue shook her head in frustration. "It's beginning to seem stupid even to me, but they're determined, even with knowing that I've already lost them the original four thousand dollars they sent me to Philadelphia with. I'd like to know what happened to that money. These people think they're going to catch the thief and get every penny back."

"Do you?"

"I have no idea what to think any longer. I've worked hard, Keeley. I don't want to do this anymore."

"But now everybody else does."

"That's what they're telling me, and they want me to lead them. God!" she burst out. "Like I'm some kind of an army general or something." She shook her head, looking dismayed. "I think it's because they're so sure they'll catch him. I think they want a lynching. They talk about it a lot. Especially Hawk Blackbean."

"He would." Keeley reread the note, then said, "You could squeeze in one or two more dances and bake sales, but I don't know if people will want to come to them too much longer. It's pretty late in the season. It won't be long before the snow piles up."

"I'd like you to keep helping me, Keeley, just like

you've been doing all along." Prue's voice was pleading.

"You know how I hate wearing that wretched dress, Prue. I can't hardly iron it good, and my feet blister up from the shoes every time."

Prue reached across the table, resting her hand on Keeley's. "I like you there. I feel safe when we're counting the money."

"Hawk's there, ain't he?" Prue's hand was warm. She hadn't touched Keeley in weeks. Keeley had made no effort to touch her either, though it had been one of the hardest things she'd ever demanded of herself. Maybe now was the time to ask her question.

"Hawk is a good man," Prue said, shattering Keeley's pleasant thoughts like shards of glass. Jealously filled her, and she squelched it. If she was going to talk to Prue about coming to live with her, she didn't want to seem mad while she was asking. Smiling politely, she said, "Forget Hawk for a minute, Prue. I got something I been thinking about for a long time."

Prue's eyes bore dark smudges beneath them. She seemed worried to the point of despair, and Keeley noticed how badly her hands shook. "What is it?"

"Prue." Keeley covered Prue's hand with her own. "You're worn out and looking ragged. You been looking kind of peaked since the bell was stole. You need somebody to look out for you. Kind of take care of you. You've done a lot for Omaha. Seems like we could take care of you for a change."

"Omaha's been good to me, Keeley, but I don't need taking care of."

"Sure you do, Prue. You could have a real quiet

life if you wanted and not have to worry about anything. Other people, the school, the church, collecting
up food and clothes for the poor folks hereabouts.
That damn bell ... It's time you took a rest."

"It is a thought, and I would love a nap right
now."

"You could come live with me, Prue." Keeley
hurried to get through this. "You could sleep in the
morning and cook just for me instead of the whole
darned town. And you could work in the garden
weeding and hoeing and watering, and nobody would
be asking something of you and expecting you to do
something for them. It'd be good for you, Prue. You
could rest."

Prue was staring at her. Hard. Keeley couldn't tell
what she was thinking. Prue withdrew her hand,
dropping it to her lap. She stood and came around to
where Keeley sat, slipping her arms around Keeley's
neck. Through her warm, blue wool dress, Keeley
could feel Prue's breasts pushing softly against her.
Prue pressed her lips against Keeley's neck. Keeley's
breath caught as her heartbeat soared.

Prue let her go and sat again as Keeley, barely
breathing, hoped her pounding heart couldn't be
heard. "You're very sweet, Keeley," Prue said softly,
"and it's quite a thought. Funny, Hawk Blackbean said
almost the same thing to me just the other day."

Keeley's face hardened. "The other day?"

"We went driving for a while last Monday afternoon. It was a beautiful day."

"Hawk Blackbean, huh? There's better out there
for you."

"Oh, I don't ride only with him. I've gone with a
few others."

154

"And?"

"And what? We ride, I come home."

"What about Hawk Blackbean?"

"What about him?"

"He hangs around a whole lot. Even keeps his hair combed and his clothes clean, anymore. Town don't even recognize him. He's sweet on you, Prue." *Like I am,* she longed to add.

"He's just a little boy, Keeley. I need more than that."

"How about a good home where you'd be safe all the time?"

Prue nodded dreamily. "Yes, I'd like that, and one day, I'll have it." She turned her eyes to Keeley. "All in good time, Keeley."

"But, what about what I said?"

"I take your words very seriously, Keeley. Very seriously indeed." The door bell tinkled, and several people came in at once.

Keeley pulled on her hat. "I'll see you later." There wouldn't be any more time to talk about this.

"I'd like that," Prue said. She flipped her hand lightly and stepped behind the counter where new patrons had parked themselves.

As Keeley mounted up, she considered how frequently Hawk Blackbean, suspected killer and thief, showed up at Prue's restaurant. She wondered if Blackbean might not be the bell thief. They'd hang him from the bell cord itself if he were, and Keeley would be right there happily yanking on the hemp until his heels quit kicking the air beneath his feet. Maybe Prue thought he was nothing but a little boy, but those who'd lived here as long as Keeley had knew better.

That night she rode to town, leaving Jingles tethered well out on the prairie. It was a very dry winter this year, the snow not more than four feet deep on the prairie and only a couple of feet deep in Omaha. Everybody was glad for the mild weather, and even now, in February, it was still easy to travel the roads.

Surreptitiously, Keeley entered Omaha bundled against the cold winter nights she would have to endure until she spotted someone pinning a note to Prue's door, or any other door. Then, by God, she'd nail the bugger. If Prue might be coming to live with her, Keeley was eager to help her in any way she could to encourage her along. Attie was going to regret being so stubborn.

Keeley spent the next several nights from dark until just before dawn broke, keeping to the shadows, moving between alleys, watching from different angles, climbing up stairs and onto roofs where, unseen, she could safely observe the streets below. She stayed fairly warm by carrying small, heated soapstones in her pockets for her hands and smaller slabs wrapped in a thick layer of cloth tied around her waist next to her skin. Why others weren't also watching for suspicious goings-on at night was a mystery to her. Or, she thought, perhaps they already were, and she just didn't see them.

Two weeks rolled by without incident. This is for Prue, Keeley told herself as her teeth chattered and her face grew numb with cold, for the woman who would one day soon come to live with her and cook for her while Keeley hunted horses for them both. One day, from among those mustangs she captured, she was going to find one that would be a good runner. On it, she would buy her way out of Omaha and into a better life. And Prue would be right there with her.

Her heart lurched. Attie should be there, not Prue, but Attie wouldn't even see her.

Keeley had returned to Attie's but always stopped near the woods, staying in the saddle while Jingles pawed at the snow and snorted clouds of steam. She watched Attie hang clothes in the cold wind, wanting to help her and knowing she couldn't because Attie would come after her with that damned switch. It didn't hurt her, but Jingles objected mightily to its stinging blows.

She dragged her attention back to her task. It'd be a wonder if Omaha could survive all this. A lot of money was going to leave the area. Even now it was hurting the stores and shops. Men were tighter in buying supplies. Women weren't purchasing as many doodads. Children weren't buying penny candy.

This night was particularly cold and windy. Snow blew directly into her face as she lay face down, peeking over the roof of Sumner's Haberdashery located across the street from Prue's establishment.

Necessity finally demanded that she rest her eyes for just a moment. She was so tired she could barely think, calculating that she had slept only ten hours in the last two days and probably less since she started acting like a sneaking vigilante on what was beginning to feel like a fool's errand. Having paid little attention as to how she tied them on tonight, the soapstones around her middle were poking her stomach a good one, but the heat they emitted was comforting. She pulled one of the stones from her pocket. It had cooled to a warm pleasantness. Positioning it between her sleeve and face, she rested her cheek against its smooth, powdery surface. One minute, she thought. She could rest one minute. In two weeks, there hadn't been one sign of the bellnapper.

She counted to sixty, then raised her head and looked at Prue's door. Nothing. She rested for another count of sixty and then two more. It was during the last that she dozed off.

While she was catnapping beneath the moon's dim light, someone quietly tacked a note to Prue's front door.

Chapter Fifteen

The sky had cleared; the moon cast bright shadows. It was possible to see without a lantern. Keeley cursed herself, her laziness, the bell thief — *especially* the bell thief — and her exhaustion as she scrambled off the roof and down the stairs.

"Why in hell I care I don't know," she growled, dashing across the street. She looked frantically around for movement as she snatched the note from the door.

A rough voice, thick with congestion hoarsely cried, "Caught him, by God!" Two hands grabbed her from behind and threw her to the ground as handily as one might throw a sack of grain from a brawny shoulder. The note went flying into the night air.

She landed with a crash, gouging her shoulder against the frozen, wagon-rutted ground. She tried to stand, but someone crashed on top of her, driving the air from her lungs. A heavy body wearing a thick sheepskin coat covered her chest and face so that drawing a breath was nearly impossible. If she didn't get this maniac off her in the next few seconds, she'd smother to death.

With strength born of panic, she arched her back as her mind began to cloud. She threw off the terrible weight and struggled to her knees. Feet pounded toward her as the coat again rammed into her, flattening her back to the earth.

"I caught the son-of-a-bitch," a voice croaked. "I got 'im!" Keeley finally recognized him. Hawk Blackbean, sounding sicker than a puppy, lay sprawled across her body.

She managed to turn her face enough to breathe, then felt a fist plow into her side as he delivered a savage blow against her ribs. He screamed and rolled off her, clutching his fist against his coat. "He's wearing iron. Watch out!"

A dozen men circled Keeley. Bright as the night was, someone had the sense to bring along a lantern. He held it near Keeley's face as she struggled to sit upright, sputtering, "You fool, Hawk Blackbean. You hit my soapstones." Her voice came out raspy and low, but he heard her.

"Keeley!" His mouth fell open.

Unsteadily, she struggled to her feet. "And if you ever hit me again, I'm gonna shoot you down like a dog." She remained bent over, still sucking wind and waiting for her painful side to ease up.

The men surrounding them backed off, expressing genuine surprise. The bearer of the lamp lowered it, saying, "My God, Hawk, you hit a woman."

"Yeah, Hawk," she said, still feeling the effects of airless lungs, a bruised shoulder and the blow that had driven the soapstone into her ribs. "I didn't put that note there. *You* did."

Hawk's head spun toward the men, at the moonlit sky, back to Keeley's scorching gaze. "You're crazy. I didn't put no note on no door. For all I know, anybody here right now could have done it — including you."

Angry curses and decisive shouts of denial gushed forth from several others. "Damn you, Blackbean," Skinny Miller said through his whistling teeth. "They's none of us here low enough to steal our own bell. And by God, I ain't never been blamed for stealing cows, neither."

Hawk fought to draw his gun hidden by his coat. "I'll shoot you for that, Miller."

Suddenly Sheriff Butts was there grabbing Blackbean's wrist, yelling in his face as Keeley breathed a sigh of relief. "Nobody here accused you of anything, Hawk, so let go of that sidearm."

With that, Prudence Jane Restaurant's door opened. "What are you men doing here at this hour? And yelling in front of my front door. Do you know that it's one o'clock in the morning?" She wore her nightgown — the one she wore on the train, Keeley saw — with her coat drawn tightly around her. She sounded as angry as a wet cat as she looked disgustedly at the whole bunch of them. "And a good half of you are drunk. Go on home where you belong.

161

You're going to give my place a bad name. Go on now, all of you."

"There's been another note, Prue," Hawk said.

Prue stepped outside, drawing the door shut behind her. "Where is it?"

"Around here someplace," Keeley answered hurriedly. She started to search the ground. "Hawk knocked it out of my hand. He says I wrote it." She was half-scared somebody might actually believe him.

"Oh, don't be ridiculous, Keeley," Prue answered. "No one believes you did it." She made no attempt to be kind or patient.

"Settle down, Delaney. We'll find it." Butts' voice seemed to steady them all. "Heywood, get that damn lantern out of my face and find that letter."

Heywood scouted the ground and quickly retrieved the message. Out of respect for Prue, he handed it to her. "Here you are, ma'am."

He held the lantern high while she read aloud: *"One week. All the money. I will tell you where to send it."* Still holding the note, she dropped her hand to her side and turned from them. Everyone stood as still as grave markers until Prue faced them again. "We're almost there, gentlemen, and lady," she added. Keeley heard a couple of snickers. She *hated* this town. "One hundred and two dollars to go," Prue said. "We will get our bell, and if we ever find him, God help the man who took it. And leave Keeley alone," she concluded, glaring at the group one more time before going inside where she quickly disappeared within the darkened interior.

Keeley wanted desperately to follow her, but Prue didn't seem to be in the mood to have anybody follow her. She whirled on Hawk. "And just how did you get here so fast, Blackbean, if you didn't write that note, huh?" Her jaw jutted out so far she felt it brush his coat. She pulled back but not before he clipped her chin with a gloved fingertip. "Back up, Delaney. I been watching this place for weeks."

She brushed away his imaginary punch, saying, "I ain't seen you, and I been here too."

Butts shook his head, threw up his hands and walked away. Keeley heard him mutter, "Nothing but a couple of damned fool babies." The others either headed home or returned to the saloons that would remain open for another couple of hours.

Clouds had moved in, quickly darkening the night to an inky blackness. Golden blocks of light shone through saloon windows. Keeley was ready to go home. The note had been delivered. By now, whoever did it was long gone. As she turned away, Hawk started in on her again.

"You are one absolutely headstrong female that ought to grow up and settle down before you —"

She spat on the ground and continued walking out of town toward Jingles, leaving Hawk still jabbering at her. His hoarse voice was nicely carried away by the growing wind. She would continue to help Prue with the dances, but she was going to quit watching the town too. That job was just too hard on her.

Chapter Sixteen

The last of the money was finally made. By mid-March, the town collected a total of $15,000. Speculation continued to run high on who had stolen the bell. During a heated argument over whose fault it was and who had more right to say "*My* bell," two men shot each other. Fortunately, both survived, but it just proved to Omaha that things were getting sorely out of control.

The *Omaha Penny Press* announced to the community that the ransom goal had been met. They were now waiting for final instructions from the Bell Thief.

At some point over the months, the thief's name had become capitalized in the paper, as though he had attained great importance. Keeley supposed he had, or soon would with $15,000 in his pocket.

She thought it exceedingly foolish on Bill Taylor's part to announce weekly in bold print how much cash the bell had collected. There was nothing like inviting trouble. Colorado, Oklahoma, Texas and Wyoming weren't that far away, and according to Taylor's newspaper, men were still being hanged these days for horse theft, killing and robbery, and robbery included banks. And no place was too far to travel if you had a good horse.

Although Attie still kept her at bay, Keeley continued to ride over almost every week. On this Sunday, a cold but clear day, and one that lifted her spirits, she thought she might bring along some crops that Attie had planted last spring — and Keeley had harvested alone last fall. The vegetables belonged to Attie as much as they did to her, maybe more so since Attie had done most of the gardening.

In the barn, beneath a great heap of hay, Keeley dug down deep, retrieving turnips, potatoes, squash and onions. They were beginning to show age, but with the right seasonings, they'd still taste good. She bagged the food in a feed sack, then tied it to the saddle. She reached Attie's woods at ten A.M. She dismounted and strapped on snowshoes before shouldering the nearly forty-pound sack and trekking to the house. The added weight she carried made the quarter-mile between her and the house look a long way off.

She hoped Attie wouldn't come charging at her with that aggravating switch. The whippings left her embarrassed and ashamed, but she wouldn't take the switch from Attie's hand. Attie was plenty mad, and Keeley believed it her duty to let Attie cool off in her own way and in her own time. But Keeley wished she'd hurry up about it.

She made it to the house without incident. Attie was taking good care of herself and her animals. The shed was strong, the animals in good shape.

Keeley set down the sack at the door and removed the snowshoes. Smoke rose serenely from the chimney. A well-tromped path was beaten between the house, woodpile and backhouse. Snow had been shoveled away from the door. Keeley's heart ballooned with hope for a warm reception. Before she could knock, the door opened a crack.

"Yes, Keeley?"

Keeley's face split into a wide grin. "I come to visit." The door didn't move.

"I can see that."

"You didn't come out with a switch."

"No, not this time."

"I . . . I brought you some garden goods," she stammered, rapidly losing her confidence. Attie brushed a loose strand of hair from her forehead, an endearing gesture that continued to enchant Keeley. An old familiar ache welled up within her. Gently, softly, she asked, "May I come in, Attie?"

Attie hesitated before opening the door. Keeley retrieved the sack and set it inside. She removed her hat, holding it uneasily with both hands.

The room was warm and as comfortable as Keeley first remembered it. Three lines of laundry stretched from one end to the other. "Place still looks the same,

Attie." Keeley attempted a smile, but Attie dismissed it as she disappeared behind a lady's blouse.

Leaving her hat on the table, Keeley unbuttoned her coat and made her way through the laundry. She followed Attie to the sink where more clothing soaked in a steaming tub. Attie fished around in the water until she grabbed a sock, then vigorously scrubbed it against a washboard.

"Not much changes in life," Attie said as she tossed the sock into a tub of rinse water. She plunged for another piece of apparel. "A few surprises to make you wonder what's going to happen next, but otherwise every day it's the same old thing from morning to night."

Keeley watched Attie's strong hands, red and raw, scrub the heavily soiled elbow of a gray shirt a dozen times before giving it a good squeeze and dropping it into the waiting tub.

"You don't sound like your old self, Attie."

"I ain't my old self, Keeley. I'm grown up now."

Keeley reached to touch Attie's hair. "You were grown up before."

Attie pulled away. "I thought I was, but I know better now."

Keeley withdrew her hand and stepped back. She pulled over the chair and sat to watch. "How's that?"

"I don't trust anybody to take care of me. I did when I was with you, but I was wrong. I should have been taking care of my own self like I've always done. Like I'm doing now."

Keeley rested her elbows on her knees and studied the cracks of the wide-plank floor that had been laid since Keeley had last been here. She wondered who

Attie had hired to do the job. "Is that what I done, Attie? Took care of you?"

"Too much. I thought my life was set. I'm at fault. I was looking for something that just wasn't there. I don't know what I expected, but it don't exist. Not in my life, it don't." Her hands stopped their incessant scrubbing. The room grew very still except for the occasional snapping and popping of wood burning in the stove. "I was wrong."

Tears glazed Keeley's eyes. She'd brought Attie to this. She loved Attie in a way that wasn't permanent like Attie must have thought it was supposed to be. "I ain't no husband, Attie. I ain't no man to marry."

""No, you ain't, Keeley. That was my mistake. I thought that part didn't matter. That we could live like husband and wife. I thought we had that strong a tie to each other." She looked at Keeley. Her eyes were dry and, Keeley thought, without hope — for herself or for them.

"I never told you I loved you, Attie," Keeley said defensively. "I never once said such words as that."

"No, you never did. And neither did I, but sometimes I thought you loved me, and I sure knew I loved you. But," Attie said, pushing aside that wayward strand of hair, "no more I don't."

Attie's words staggered Keeley. She remained still for a long moment, long enough to let the aching throb subside within her chest. "I should have said the words, then. I thought them often enough, but figuring I was a girl, I didn't have the right to tell you I loved you."

"Loved me?"

"Yes," Keeley whispered.

"Then . . . you don't now."

"I didn't say that. I never said that, Attie. I never told you I didn't love you, neither."

Attie turned back to her work. "That's true. You didn't."

Keeley hung her head, wishing it would fall off and roll out the door so that she could end her misery. "I should have. I didn't know what to do. How to behave. I don't know about stuff like that."

"Me either, Keeley. I could have done the same. You know, told you. Maybe then, we'd have done better."

"I thought we were doing okay, Attie."

"Prue got in your way."

"No, she didn't!" Keeley stood angrily. "You always thought that, and it ain't true."

"I know better."

"No, you don't know any such thing, Attie Webster. You're making it up. You just don't want anything more to do with me, I'm thinking, and you're using Prue as an excuse." She pulled on her hat saying, "I better be going home."

Attie shook the suds from her hands and grabbed Keeley by the ears. She pulled Keeley's face to hers, kissing her soundly and lingering there until Keeley melted in Attie's arms.

Keeley's heart filled with renewed hope that they could work things out. She reached to put her arms around Attie's waist, but Attie pulled away and said, "Good-bye, Keeley. Don't come back here, ever again."

Keeley dropped her arms. Her body felt tingly all over as fear gripped her. "Attie . . ."

"I mean it, Keeley. I don't want you here anymore. That was my good-bye kiss to you. I don't want you bothering me anymore."

"But . . . but you just kissed me."

"I take care of myself now, Keeley. I wanted to be sure I wasn't making a mistake for myself. I wasn't. Don't come here anymore."

Keeley remained rooted to the spot, her jaw working but no words coming out. How could Attie do this to her?

"Go, Keeley. Now." Attie ducked under the laundry and opened the door. The air was bitter, but she seemed not to care that the place would become stone-cold if Keeley didn't leave instantly.

Fighting tears, Keeley walked proudly out the door and strapped on her snowshoes. She'd be damned if she'd look at Attie. The door closed firmly.

She hiked back to Jingles and mounted up, talking to him all the way back to her farm. "Tell me, Jingles, how do I feel about Attie's quitting me for good? Huh? How did all this happen, anyway? When, horse? Tell me that. And when did Attie decide she was better off alone than with me? You can't answer that one either, can you, old fellow? She as much as called me a liar too. You know what I wish? I wish to God I had never taken that train trip with Prue Morris. That's what I wish for most of all, Jingles. That's what I wish for most of all."

She spurred the slowing animal and squinted heavily against the glaring sun bouncing off the brilliant white snow. She tugged her hat lower over her face to fight off the pain in her eyes that she insisted was being caused by the dazzling whiteness.

Chapter Seventeen

Keeley's days blended together, one into the other as snow whipped across the plains and piled high against her buildings. She stayed busy splitting wood, shoveling snow and making sure her stock, now stabled, was fed.

Carefully choosing her timing, Keeley ventured to town less often these days. The normal hour-and-a-quarter ride now took two hours or better. When she traveled, she made sure the snow covering was frozen enough so that Jingles sank only a few inches into its crusted, sun-blinding surface and that good weather looked promising for the day.

She left early in the morning, staying long enough to complete her errands and catch up on all the latest news by reading old copies of the *Omaha* that Prue had hanging around her restaurant. She also listened to any gossip she could garner from Prue or others, but she was most anxious to hear if the bell's ransom had been delivered. Before returning home, she'd have a bite to eat as she gazed at the color of Prue's blue eyes and the silvery, yellow glow of her hair. She'd study the delicate lips that had once kissed her own and inhale the delicious odors of baking pies and cakes while recalling the night Prue lay in her arms and then remember the many nights that Attie had lain in them too. By then she would have become so torn inside, she would angrily toss her money on the counter and return home, brooding all the way about the loss of both women. She'd wonder who she loved more, Attie or Prue, for she knew she loved them both. Equally, or not, she could never decide. She knew with a dead certainty that it was killing her to think about it.

Thus, winter ended, and new growth hit the plains with bright, colorful madness. With glorious vengeance, spring cast aside her wintery, white blanket and puffed out her earthly bosom. The fertile land grew thick with a rush of rich green grasses, so healthy that the blades sometimes looked almost blue. Meadowlarks sang; flowers arrogantly flaunted their array of colors; freshly plowed soil intoxicated farmers anew; ranchers felt the promise of exceedingly fat cattle. Women, freed at last from children getting underfoot throughout the cold months, planted large gardens near their homes, while their offspring went just a little insane, happily unleashed after having been confined indoors for longer than any child ought to be.

Keeley awoke with the smell of the new season filling her nostrils and the sound of heavy water rushing pell-mell through the creek. Cat-like, she stretched and rose. She dressed, then consumed a huge, leisurely breakfast of bacon, eggs, fried potatoes and coffee. She saddled Jingles and headed for Omaha, needing a few things before taking off for the plains to search for her first bunch of mustangs this spring. Those captured last fall had fattened well. They were settled and would be easy to work. She needed only a few more head to complete her next herd. The fort might be shy of good ponies by now. Soldiers went out on maneuvers throughout winter whether there were problems or not, just to stay in training. They often wore out their mounts in the process. And, too, horses unexpectedly died.

Mild though it had been, winter had dragged on endlessly. Keeley wanted to get out and ride beneath the warm sun. She was convinced that this was the year she would find a great racer, one that would beat all other horses put together. She was certain because she had encountered him last fall. By her estimation, the bay had run a quarter-mile in thirty seconds or less. He was fast, so fast that within minutes he had quickly outdistanced Jingles and could easily have beaten Hawk's horse. When she realized it would be impossible to outrun the stallion, Keeley had pulled up and watched a long trail of dust string out behind him. With a gleam in her eye and the corners of her mouth pulled up in a grim but determined smile, she'd said, "You're laughing at me now, horse, but come spring, you're mine."

Now on her way to town, foremost in her mind was the thought that tomorrow she was going after that horse. In two years' time, she'd be shed of Omaha and lonesome thoughts of Prue and Attie. She'd live somewhere where the weather and people were a whole lot kinder to a body than they were here.

A formidable hunger to see Attie struck her. She fought the compelling inclination for a couple of miles, then turned eastward toward the Missouri.

From the woods, she stared longingly at Attie's small house. The horse and wagon were missing. Likely she was delivering laundry. Maybe she'd gone into Omaha, and Keeley would be lucky enough to see her there.

Regrettably, Keeley hadn't thought the way Attie had, hadn't dreamed the same way. She had taken it for granted that Attie would always be there, like the rocks were always in the creek or the clouds were there every time it rained. Tears threatened her scowling eyes as she reined toward town.

Because she had been to town so infrequently since January, men, women and some of the older children as well, looked her over with a critical eye until they realized who she was. She felt the town's tension then. In the hardware store she learned that the bell thief had been quiet for months, and the ransom still sat in the bank. No doubt, winter had kept him hobbled like it had most everybody else. With the weather change, she expected trouble to begin anew.

Hoping to see Attie, she hung around town until

evening shadows lengthened and the air had cooled considerably. The streets and sidewalks gradually emptied, but Attie never appeared. As she left Omaha, Keeley fixed her sights on a small, thin brown dog running across the rutted main street.

"Maybe I should get me a pup, Jingles. He could stay in the soddy and keep me company and look at me mournful when I ate. I could slip him food under the table and make believe Ma was there to scold me. Maybe Pa and Aaron could hunt . . . *Damn!*" she yelled into the fading light of day. She was going *nuts!*

Several people looked her way as she bellowed to the sky. "That you, Delaney?" a shadowed face asked. Mike Decker, a cowboy from Tom Appleton's ranch, stepped off the sidewalk.

"It's me, Mike." She noted he wore a gun.

"What you yelling about? You trying to scare folks?" His burred voice was angry and accusing.

Keeley rode over to the tall cowpuncher. "I'm just feeling good. Change in the weather and all."

"Well, feel good someplace else, Keeley. The town's nerved up enough as it is."

She dismounted asking, "What's up? The bell thief show up in the last five minutes?"

"No, and he ain't going to, either, if I have anything to do with it." His hand dropped to his weapon.

Thoughtfully, Keeley scratched the hair beneath her hat, then looked steadily into Mike's eyes. "How much money did you put into the bell, Mike?"

"I ain't got to tell you anything, Delaney."

"No, sir, you don't. I was just wondering. You know, concerned about you."

"Ha."

"And about everybody else here. We all got money

in the bell, Mike. Right? And if not money, then time." Eric Anderson, a balding, broad-chested rancher, joined them, accompanied by two men Keeley didn't recognize. Undaunted, she continued on. "You never came to any of my family's funerals. Not a one of you. Not a man, woman or child. Not even a dog showed up when my people died, Mike. Now, I think that's as unkind as a town can be, but that's how Omaha is, I guess. Always looking out for its own self and forgetting everybody else. But I'll tell you something, Mike, and you can spread it around town if you want to. I hate this place for that, except for just a body or two. You all don't give a damn about anybody unless he's a man running a ranch or a farm or else lives in town. But, Mike . . ." She stepped close to him. "I put time into that bell. I worked to help make money to buy it and to bring it to town. And I went after it too."

"And you lost it on the way, Delaney," Anderson said. "Maybe you took it someplace. Made a deal with somebody on the railroad to sidetrack it someplace."

Recognizing his accusations for the stupidity they were, she went on as though he hadn't spoken. "I don't have any money, so I put in time, Mike."

"Why bother if you hate us so much?" Mike stepped back. The others shuffled their feet, letting him speak for them, it seemed.

"Because I wanted to do something for Prue Morris. She's always doing for this town. What'd you ever do for her?"

"We all gave money."

"And I gave time. So we all did something. That

makes us like one, like a single family going for a bell. Trouble is, it didn't work out that way. Everybody got mad at everybody else. Couple of men got hurt." She didn't mention Hawk's fist plowing into her ribs and hurting her during that nightly stakeout. "Everybody looking at everybody else out the sides of their eyes." She turned her head and stared into the night. "This town is a sorry lot for not pulling together when they should. Now go spread that around town."

"I will, Delaney. Anybody ever tell you, you talk too damn much?"

"A time or two." She left them and instead of continuing homeward led Jingles toward Prue's, wondering what had possessed her to speak out so.

By now it had grown completely dark. The restaurant was closed Monday evenings. It was the one night of the week Prue rested, but Keeley desperately needed to see a friendly face. Maybe Prue would talk with her for a few minutes.

She took the back stairs to Prue's apartment. Keeley had never been up there. She was excited as she knocked quietly on the door. Through the window, she could see a lantern burning on a small kitchen table. She waited, then softly knocked a second time. Prue's shadow passed in front of the window, then faded from sight. Apparently, she didn't hear Keeley. Not wanting to rap louder, Keeley reached for the knob and opened the door an inch or two. "Prue?"

She entered a small kitchen. A sink was to the left with cupboards built overhead with a pie cupboard on the opposite wall; chairs were neatly pushed beneath a linen-covered table.

She removed her hat and stepped inside. As she did, her toe struck something. A couple of suitcases and carpetbags were parked near the door. She didn't know about the suitcases, but the carpetbags looked stuffed to capacity.

She closed the door behind her, keeping her hand on the knob, clutching it to hold herself up. She leaned against the door's honest solidness, afraid to speculate upon what the luggage might mean.

Prue froze as she came out of the bedroom. "Keeley!"

"Thought I'd drop in for a minute." Keeley tried to mask her confusion and pain. "Looks like you're going on a trip."

Quickly recovering herself, Prue asked, "How are you, Keeley? Please, sit a moment." She pulled out a chair and turned up the lantern, then lighted another by the sink. "I didn't hear you come in."

"I knocked. Twice."

"Well, I'm glad you're here," Prue said brightly. She picked up the lamp and joined Keeley. Nervously, her hands caressed the tablecloth. "But I have to admit that I'm quite busy this evening. My one night off, you know." She looked sincerely apologetic. "We can chat for a minute or two. But no longer." She pointed a playful, slender finger at her watch.

Keeley knew she was being told to leave. "When will you be back?"

Before Prue could reply, she was interrupted by a light knock on the door. She rose to answer it, giving Keeley a weak grin as she passed her chair.

Keeley was beginning to feel mighty uncomfortable about the way Prue was behaving. If Hawk Blackbean showed up, she'd kick him all the way down the stairs and across the Missouri.

"I got here as soon as I could," came the voice from behind the door.

Keeley whirled. "Attie!" The chair screeched loudly against the floor as she rose. "Attie," she repeated.

Prue said flatly, "She showed up a few minutes ago."

Attie stepped inside. "No matter."

"We were hoping to avoid this with you, Keeley," Prue said.

"Avoid what?" Blood raced through Keeley's veins. Her head throbbed. She could hear her pulse surging rhythmically in her ears.

"Attie is going to visit with me for a while this evening," Prue said.

Keeley looked at the baggage and then at the two women. "I don't believe you. You're leaving, Prue, and you're taking my Attie with you."

The door shut with a vicious bang, and Attie exploded. "I'm not 'your' Attie. We already talked about this."

"We didn't talk about it enough. I was wrong."

"You bet you were, Keeley Delaney. Prue told me what happened on the train."

"Oh Lord, Attie." She appealed to Prue for help. "Tell her, Prue. Tell her that nothing happened on the train."

"I told her exactly what happened, Keeley. I thought she had a right to know."

"Kissing, touching each other. Screaming out loud like you done with me," Attie shouted, her hands punctuating each accusing word.

"Screaming? Prue told you I was screaming? On a train with people all around us?" Keeley inhaled deeply. "Not likely, Attie. Use your head."

"Then you admit that you and her was making love."

"We were not! Prue, tell her. I wasn't screaming, and we didn't make any love. Now *tell* her." Keeley slammed her palm against the tabletop. "You got me crazy, Prue. What did you tell her, anyway?"

"Just the truth, Keeley. She came to my door last fall and asked."

"Last fall?"

"Yes. And I told her all about us."

"There ain't no *us*, Prue. There never has been."

"Tell Attie that."

"I've told her and told her."

"Well, it seems as though she doesn't believe you." Keeley sank to the chair.

"Why don't we all sit?" Prue said and pointedly joined Keeley. Attie followed suit.

"I don't believe you, Keeley," Attie confirmed. "And I'm leaving with Prue."

"But why?"

"We both need a little vacation," Prue said. She rested her hand over Attie's.

Keeley turned sick, her stomach instantly boiling with nausea as she stared at the two hands clasped together on the table. "Why?" she whispered. "Why?"

"Because," Prue said matter-of-factly, "we love each other. We've told each other so, and we're going off to enjoy ourselves for a few months."

"But . . . what about the bell? What about how hard you worked to bring it here?"

"It'll get here, Keeley. I'm sure everything will

work out. But I told you once before, I'm tired of the whole thing. Let someone else do it now."

Keeley's mind whirled with dull confusion. She thought she might faint and never get up again — never *want* to get up. Prue and Attie, leaving — together! "When you going?" she asked.

Prue checked her watch. "In half an hour. The Northern Pacific."

The very same train that she and Prue had taken. Keeley's head dropped until her chin rested against her chest. "No way to change your minds?"

"None," Attie said.

"Well, I sure as hell can't chase after you, Attie," Keeley retorted. "I ain't got any money, except for ten dollars. And I still owe Prue a hundred and fifteen dollars." She looked questioningly at Attie. "And just how are you paying for your ticket, Miss Attie?"

Prue answered for her. "I bought Attie's ticket, Keeley. She'll be well taken care of."

"Taken care of. Well now, ain't that funny, Attie? That's exactly what you didn't want from me. What changed your mind?"

"I don't want to work anymore, just like you don't. And I'm not going to."

"You gonna just walk out on your business too, Prue, and all the friends you made here in Omaha and the people who believe in you?"

"Timmy's in charge. He'll take care of them. Besides, it's just a vacation."

Keeley rose. "Then I guess it's time for me to leave. Nothing left to say." Her heart skipped a couple of beats, and her head swam as she put on her hat. Why did she feel like she would never again see either of these women? Even now as they were about to desert her, as they were about to become lovers and maybe already were, she still loved them both. Her voice was unsteady as she asked, "Can I carry your bags for you ladies? I don't want to go with bad feelings left between us," although she knew she'd have plenty once her shock wore off. Without waiting for an answer, she picked up a carpetbag.

Prue leaped for it, nearly ripping it from Keeley's grasp. Gruffly, she said, "We can manage, Keeley. Thank you."

Keeley quickly released the bag out of sheer surprise. Now why would Prue act like that? Keeley had watched her give up her satchel to a half-dozen different people during her and Keeley's travels, and most of them strangers. Her brows drew together as she puzzled over Prue's behavior. Prue was breathing heavily, the bag still clutched to her breast. Keeley narrowed her eyes as she asked, "You got that ransom money in there, Prue?" Prue was so bent on recovering this bell that she would do something like this and not tell a soul. "Is that why you're going off? You're delivering the ransom yourself, ain't you? The money's been in your name in the bank. You could take it out any time you want, and the bank can't say a word. Can't even talk about it. Attie, are you part of this plan? You gonna get paid for this foolishness? I hope it's plenty." She spoke quickly, thinking quickly. She was wrong about Attie and Prue. They weren't going on a vacation. They were going to pay off a thief. She smiled, her face brightening until her cheeks ached. "You're getting the bell back, and this leaving stuff is all fake, ain't it? But you girls can't do this. You could get shot! Where's Sheriff Butts? He should be doing this. Men should be doing this." Keeley reached to snatch back the bag as her admiration for Prue soared to heady heights. Such courage in a woman, such determination. And her little Attie, going right along to help. This was an excellent cover. No one in the world would guess that two small women would carry such a large amount of cash with them. But using women made the whole plan insane. "I'm going to go see Butts. This ain't right of him." She had completely barred from her mind Prue and Attie's admitted love for each other.

"You say anything to anyone, Keeley, and you're going to mess up a well laid-out plan." Prue again reclaimed the bag, hanging onto it. "Now just go on home, and leave me to my work."

Renewed pain ricocheted around Keeley's brain, and all that she had hoped for became unraveled as the awful truth finally and firmly sank in. Prue actually *was* skipping town. And Attie was going too. Prue had plenty of money for them both, and *damn it to hell*, they loved each other.

Keeley looked steadily at Prue Morris, the woman most loved and trusted by everyone in Omaha and its surrounding territory. "How'd you pull it off, Prue? What'd you do, feed the bank some line about how another note showed up, and you and only you were supposed to deliver the ransom? There never was going to be a bell, was there? You been lying since you brought yourself to Omaha, and faking tears and sorrow all along so's we'd collect up even more money with that fake bell idea. And somehow you stuck up all the notes too, didn't you? Boy, you are a clever one." She gripped the back of a chair. "That man, Mr. Bacheller, who came to see you on the train. The one who gave you the bill of sale. You set that up so I'd witness that you paid for the bell. If I hadn't volunteered to go, I'll bet you'd have taken Blackbean. Somebody had to see how honest you were, didn't they? What'd you give Bacheller, a cashier's check already signed? I know about checks, Prue. He could put it in a bank for you. Maybe you paid him part of that money to do it?" Keeley half turned to Attie while still keeping her eyes on Prue. "She's a thief of the worse kind, Attie. She's stealing from the town. There were children that put money in the ransom pot too. You want that kind of person in your life?" Keeley faced Attie and put her hands on her shoulders. "Come with me, Attie. Right now. Don't go with her. She's wicked."

Attie twisted from Keeley's grasp. "I'm going, Keeley. I'm tired of being used and used and *used*! I'm nothing but a slave."

"You make honest money, Attie." Keeley was crying.

"Who cares about honesty? It never got me one thing that I could call my own and enjoy."

"Your house, your job . . ."

"I *need* those things. I don't enjoy them. They keep me alive. I want to have more than that. Prue can give it to me."

Keeley opened the door. "I don't believe you, Attie," and indeed, she didn't. Attie's eyes betrayed her. Keeley had always been able to tell what Attie was thinking. It used to make Attie mad as hell because she couldn't hide anything from Keeley.

"Keeley." Prue's eyes were cold as steel, and her voice was tightly controlled. She put her hand on Keeley's arm, her fingers digging into her coat. "Are you going to tell Butts?"

Keeley looked down at the beautiful hand that once made her arm smolder right through the fabric she was wearing. Now it looked skeletal. She detested its touch and peeled it from her sleeve. She asked Attie, "Are you determined to go with her?"

Attie's eyes narrowed defiantly. "I am."

"Then no, I won't say a word." Keeley heard them both release their breaths.

"Why?" they asked simultaneously.

"Nobody came to my kins' funerals. I don't owe this town one blamed thing."

On the way home, she heard the 9:30 P.M. train whistle blowing across the land.

Chapter Eighteen

Having purchased seeds and onion bulbs a couple of weeks ago, Keeley worked hard throughout May, plowing and planting, putting in a sizeable garden while loathing the drudgery of it all. She'd be needing to sell the crops or she wouldn't be able to buy enough grain and hay to feed her horses through the winter. She'd have to *can* this year too. Thoughts of all those jars and lids, the broiling heat in the soddy, the mess that would be created, made her stomach ache. As soon as she could she headed for the prairie.

For the next couple of weeks, she chased after the

mustang that would free her from working from dusk to dawn. She was closer to figuring out how the stallion thought and, daily, outwitted her, and how to be smarter than he. Another week, maybe two, and she thought she'd have him. If she built a corral at the end of that small ravine by the only creek hereabouts and he went there to drink, he'd be trapped. He couldn't escape from there. The walls were just too steep. "Soon," she said to Jingles, who nickered at the sound of her voice. "Soon."

At night on the plains while she sat before a campfire, shadows danced around her, and she stared into the mesmerizing firelight for long stretches of time. She envisioned herself in some fancy hotel someplace well south of here, her shiny new boots comfortably propped up on a green felt tabletop and a pretty woman serving her a cold beer. She thought a good deal about Prue and Attie and how they were probably already doing something similar, although she couldn't quite picture either of them with her feet on a table. But they would be where the good times were. With a total of $19,000 in their pockets, how could they not? They could live like queens for years on that kind of money. She envied them their luxurious living, imagining them owning good horses, driving fancy carriages, wearing pretty dresses, attending rich folks' parties with likely a servant or two to wait on them.

The days crawled by as she traveled far and wide gathering enough wood to build a trap for the mustang, who seemed to have disappeared into thin air. She eventually had to end her search. She needed fresh food supplies. She was sick to death of eating rabbit with no salt and drinking days' old coffee. There was also the young garden, which she had pushed herself to plant and certainly needed tending, and her fence line to check.

She made it home in five days' time. She had wandered almost halfway to Fort Niobrara, the memory of the robbery still fresh in her mind. Other than Attie, only Prue knew where she'd been going. As she thought deeper about it, now fully aware of what kind of a woman Prue was, Keeley believed with her whole being that Prue had deliberately served her bad chicken to be sure that she got sick and stayed sick, knowing she'd still travel. It was Prue, Keeley recalled, who put the chicken on each person's plate that evening. She must then have had an accomplice track Keeley all the way to Niobrara and back to see which night she would still be damn sick on her return. He picked his night and made the switch from gold to stones, leaving everything else untouched. "Every little penny Prue could get her evil hands on, she took, Jingles. One way or the other. And I worried about paying her back. What a fool I am. Bet Attie doesn't know any of this." She wondered who Prue's accomplice was and how much she had paid.

Keeley spent several days riding the fence line, repairing loose wires, resetting leaning posts, making sure the horses were well confined. She went to the river and sawed down trees, putting her mark on them so that later in the fall she could claim them and drag them home for winter fuel. The soddy had some winter damage to its outside walls, and she added new sod. By the middle of the following week she was ready to go to town and restock her supplies before going after the mustang again.

She left for Omaha that Wednesday, early the next morning. She drew up before the church just for old time's sake. On top was a belfry that hadn't been there before. She dismounted and stood staring up at it and wondered who had paid for the lumber.

As Mavis VanAllen walked by, Keeley called to him. "How come there's a belfry, Mr. VanAllen?" She liked the spry, old man, dressed in a brown cotton shirt, sleeves rolled up and baggy brown coveralls. He was one of the few who had worked for her pa on several different occasions when he had needed help. VanAllen had always spoken politely to Keeley, and Keeley liked him for that. "We still hope to get a bell someday, Miss Keeley. Come on inside. Got something to show you."

She tossed Jingles' reins over the rail and followed him in.

"Did you know that the ransom money disappeared?" VanAllen asked. Keeley felt her stomach tighten as they walked to the front of the church. "Seems our Miss Prue was the bell thief."

Keeley did her best to look shocked. "No!"

"Yep! We think that the first time she went to Philadelphia to order the bell, she never really did. Instead, we figure she paid a man at the forge out of that first four thousand we sent her with, to claim that if anybody came looking, the bell had been shipped. We also think this same person presented shipping papers to the railroad stockyard. Damn chaotic place. I used to work for the railroad. You could lose an elephant in those yards."

"Or a bell they thought was there."

"Or a bell," VanAllen agreed. "Meanwhile, when

Miss Prue went to order the bell by herself, likely she stashed the money in a bank right there in Philadelphia, instead."

"How was she supposed to pay for the bell?"

"Cashier's check made out to herself. She could request it without question since the bell account had always been in her name, and the bank couldn't mention it to anyone. We'll get her," VanAllen said. He didn't sound as though he doubted it for a moment. "We're pretty sure we know where she is."

"Maybe she didn't take the money. Maybe she just left." Keeley's palms began to sweat.

"No, she's got it all right. That little gal, Attie Webster, told Sheriff Butts how Prue took the money."

Keeley's body went numb. "Attie's here? In Omaha?"

"She lives here, don't she, over on the river somewhere?"

"Did. Does. You're right, Mr. VanAllen. She does. How'd she know about the money?"

"She saw Miss Prue get on the train with it. Said she was in town real late that night delivering laundry. Hard-working gal, that Attie Webster. Didn't know she delivered to the station. Guess she does. Anyway, Miss Prue opened the bag to buy a ticket, and she saw all the money. Said she didn't think much of it at the time because Miss Prue did pretty well with that restaurant of hers. But then Miss Attie thought about it for a day or two and decided that it was just too much money for a restaurant lady to have made selling food. That's when she went to Butts. Nope, little Miss Prue didn't bother with a cashier's check this time. She was set to travel far and fast. You can do that with a lot of cash."

"So she never left town."

"Who? Miss Attie? No, she's been right here, doing everybody's washing, day and night, just like she's always done. We need that little woman."

Like I do, Keeley thought.

VanAllen asked, "Didn't she used to stay at your soddy for a time?"

"While back, that was. She got longing for her own place, she said, and went on home."

"Um. Well, come on over here."

VanAllen sat on the front pew. "Have a seat with me, Keeley, and look here. Omaha wants to show this to you." He pointed to a new, brass plate carefully centered and tacked to the pew's backrest. Sunlight streamed through the window, striking the wood and making the metal shine like gold. She read: *In memory of Patrick and Mary Delaney and son Aaron, who gave of their lives to help enrich their community.*

Keeley looked at the old man. "I don't understand."

"Well, Keeley." The brass plate gleamed between them. He cleared his throat. "Mike Decker told me and everybody else in town what you think of us. Can't say I blame you at all, but we don't want anybody thinking that way about Omaha. We plan on being a real big city someday. A place to be proud of, that men would want to bring their families to. It's growing big in cattle and grain, and we can't have any of that if hate abides here because we been neglectful of our own folks." He rested his thin, gray-haired arm on the back of the pew. "We didn't know your people died, Keeley. We only heard about each one, one at a time, long after they were buried. We'd have been there, if we knew. Just like you were always there for us to help us raise money for the bell, and then going after it like you did, and then raising more money for it and trying to catch the thief. Well . . ." He looked ashamed.

"Why are you telling me this, Mr. VanAllen?" A hardness welled up within Keeley's heart. "This town is way too late."

"That's the thing of it, Keeley. We are too late. But you never gave up on us even when you believed we'd given up on you. You just kept coming back and coming back."

"Like some fool dog who keeps getting kicked aside."

"No, like somebody who cares about Omaha, in spite of how you say you feel about us."

Keeley pondered that for a moment. "I did it for Prue, not the town. She was my friend."

"She was everybody's friend. She was clever, that one. Worked on our good side for two years."

"And made nineteen thousand dollars for her work."

"Like I say, we'll get it back."

"What'll happen to her?"

"Jail, probably. But she's pretty clever. She might just talk her way out of it."

As furious as she was with Prue and her double-dealing ways, she hoped Prue wouldn't get caught. She had once cared too much for the beautiful Easterner whose voice sounded like bells whenever she spoke. Keeley laughed softly. "Omaha's belle really put one over on us, didn't she?"

VanAllen chuckled too. "Omaha's belle. Pretty good, Keeley. Pretty good." His smile faded. "Well,

192

anyway. This pew is in memory of your family, Keeley. We're sorry for having missed their burials. We're sorry you had to do it all by yourself."

"Next time I need help, I'll ride in and ask, Mr. VanAllen."

"Don't be burying anybody, Keeley."

"No, sir, I won't."

VanAllen nodded and stood. "It ain't Prue's restaurant anymore, but they still make some pretty good coffee over there. Mind if I buy you a cup?"

"Thanks." They wandered over to Timmy's. Apparently he owned the place, for his name hung boldly over the door.

Hawk sat on the edge of the boardwalk scratching at the dirt between his boots. Dante was parked at the rail. Blackbean wore the old greasy buckskins that Keeley was so familiar with. He glanced up with watery, bloodshot eyes as she and VanAllen drew near. His beard and hair grew in a tangled mess. Flies landed on him. He didn't bother to brush them away.

Keeley paused. "I'll be right in, Mr. VanAllen." VanAllen nodded and left her. She sat beside Hawk and draped her arms over her knees. "You're looking kind of peaked, Hawk. You okay?" He was looking like death.

He was silent for a while, then said, "She fooled us all, didn't she, Delaney?" His head drooped farther, and a tear fell from his eye. She looked away.

"She sure did, Hawk. The whole town. And friends."

Cleverly, Hawk had sketched a bell in the dirt with a twig he was fussing with. He scratched it out. "I loved her, Keeley. I thought I knew her."

Me too, she thought, and wondered why. "We all thought we knew her, Hawk." She looked around the town, studied Jingles' knees, studied Dante's knees. "I'm sorry for you, Hawk." She was sorry for herself too, for ever having felt anything for Prue Morris, liar and thief, which is what she herself had once been — the liar part, anyway. She was sure she'd be ashamed of herself for the rest of her days.

He asked, "Do you think if the bell got here, she'd have stayed?"

Keeley didn't know how to answer him. "Hawk," she said as kindly as she could. "I don't know if you heard, but she —"

He waved her off. "Yeah, I know all about it. I was just hoping like any fool would hope, I guess."

Keeley patted his shoulder as she rose. There was nothing else to say. "You take care of yourself, Hawk."

"Thanks, Delaney." He went back to scratching in the dirt.

She didn't hate him anymore. He'd gotten his comeuppance more than any man ought to.

She and VanAllen sat in the rear where Timmy's new wife, Eileen, waited on them, smiling and chatting, a sunny bubble bouncing around the room as she moved from table to table making sure customers were happy.

"Here you are, Timmy."

Keeley looked up. She'd know that voice any place on earth. Attie plunked a bulky basket of laundry onto the counter. "Towels to last you a week."

"Thanks, Miss Attie." He passed her another laden basket. "I got two shirts in there this time."

"I'll take care of them, Timmy. Be back in a week."

Keeley sat very, very still, not breathing, not moving. Now was not the time to approach Attie, but later, when her stomach had settled, and her heart had calmed. Attie carried the heaping basket outside. Through the window Keeley watched her put it into the wagon.

Keeley struggled to stay put. Attie really *was* back. What's more, people were feeling pretty bad about how they'd treated the Delaneys even though it wasn't entirely their fault. A couple of men had nodded at her just now as she came into the restaurant with VanAllen. Maybe Omaha wasn't all that bad. She'd have to think about it when she went chasing after that cussed mustang again.

She sat twisting her hands, unable to listen to VanAllen talking about the weather. Standing, she said, "Would you excuse me, Mr. VanAllen?" Before he could answer she was halfway to the door. She whipped it open and reached the wagon just as Attie clucked to the horse. "Hold on, Attie!"

Attie looked at her and hauled back on the reins. "Hello, Keeley." She didn't smile, but Keeley didn't think she seemed entirely unfriendly, either.

Keeley's heart pounded so hard it hurt. "Can we talk, Attie, just for a minute?" She could read nothing in Attie's eyes.

"I have people waiting for their laundry."

Keeley put her hand on the wagon. "I know, Attie, but I need to talk to you for just a minute. Please."

"You hurt me, Keeley."

"Come on, now, Attie. What do you think you did to me when you took off with Prue?"

"But I didn't."

"I can see that. Why didn't you tell me you were still here?"

"I've been ashamed about what I did. I couldn't face you. I as much as stole that money too, Keeley, even if I didn't go with Prue and even if I reported it, finally."

Keeley pursed her lips. "Well, me too, Attie. I knew and I didn't say anything."

"I'm trying to put it behind me. I have what I want right here in Omaha. It's enough for me. A whole lot of money ain't the answer."

"What is?"

"A good job, which I've got. It's hard work, but it's honest. And my house. I like my house. Didn't know how much until I left it." She breathed deeply, then asked, "When you leaving Omaha? You must have caught that mustang by now."

"Not so far. And" — Keeley looked at the ground — "I don't know that I will be leaving."

"Why not?"

"Maybe I like it here after all." She looked up again.

Attie asked without smiling, "Would you like to ride along with me, Keeley?"

"How far you going?"

"Oh, I don't know. How far do you think we can get today?"

Keeley didn't believe that Attie was talking about miles but about the two of them and how they could work things out. There were so many things to work out too, but she had no doubt they would succeed. "Maybe I better tie Jingles on the back."

"I think so."

Attie was smiling as Keeley climbed up beside her.

LOOKING FOR NAIAD?

Buy our books at
www.naiadpress.com

or call our toll-free number
1-800-533-1973

or by fax (24 hours a day)
1-850-539-9731

A few of the publications of
THE NAIAD PRESS, INC.
P.O. Box 10543   Tallahassee, Florida 32302
Phone (850) 539-5965
Toll-Free Order Number: 1-800-533-1973
Web Site: WWW.NAIADPRESS.COM

Mail orders welcome. Please include 15% postage.
Write or call for our free catalog which also features an
incredible selection of lesbian videos.

SILVER THREADS by Lyn Denison.208 pp. Finding her way
back to love . . .   ISBN 1-56280-231-3 $11.95

CHIMNEY ROCK BLUES by Janet McClellan. 240 pp. 4th Tru
North mystery.   ISBN 1-56280-233-X   11.95

OMAHA'S BELL by Penny Hayes. 208 pp. Orphaned Keeley
Delaney woos the lovely Prudence Morris.   ISBN 1-56280-232-1   11.95

SIXTH SENSE by Kate Calloway. 224 pp. 6th Cassidy James
mystery.   ISBN 1-56280-228-3   11.95

DAWN OF THE DANCE by Marianne K. Martin. 224 pp. A dance
with an old friend, nothing more . . . yeah!   ISBN 1-56280-229-1   11.95

WEDDING BELL BLUES by Julia Watts. 240 pp. Love, family,
and a recipe for success.   ISBN 1-56280-230-5   11.95

THOSE WHO WAIT by Peggy J. Herring. 160 pp. Two
sisters . . . in love with the same woman.   ISBN 1-56280-223-2   11.95

WHISPERS IN THE WIND by Frankie J. Jones. 192 pp. "If you
don't want this," she whispered, "all you have to say is 'stop.' "
                                            ISBN 1-56280-226-7   11.95

WHEN SOME BODY DISAPPEARS by Therese Szymanski.
192 pp. 3rd Brett Higgins mystery.   ISBN 1-56280-227-5   11.95

THE WAY LIFE SHOULD BE by Diana Braund. 240 pp. Which
one will teach her the true meaning of love?   ISBN 1-56280-221-6   11.95

UNTIL THE END by Kaye Davis. 256pp. 3rd Maris Middleton
mystery.   ISBN 1-56280-222-4   11.95

FIFTH WHEEL by Kate Calloway. 224 pp. 5th Cassidy James
mystery.   ISBN 1-56280-218-6   11.95

JUST YESTERDAY by Linda Hill. 176 pp. Reliving all the
passion of yesterday.   ISBN 1-56280-219-4   11.95

THE TOUCH OF YOUR HAND edited by Barbara Grier and
Christine Cassidy. 304 pp. Erotic love stories by Naiad Press
authors.   ISBN 1-56280-220-8   14.95

WINDROW GARDEN by Janet McClellan. 192 pp. They discover
a passion they never dreamed possible.   ISBN 1-56280-216-X   11.95

PAST DUE by Claire McNab. 224 pp. 10th Carol Ashton
mystery.   ISBN 1-56280-217-8   11.95

CHRISTABEL by Laura Adams. 224 pp. Two captive hearts and
the passion that will set them free.   ISBN 1-56280-214-3   11.95

PRIVATE PASSIONS by Laura DeHart Young. 192 pp. An
unforgettable new portrait of lesbian love . . .   ISBN 1-56280-215-1   11.95

BAD MOON RISING by Barbara Johnson. 208 pp. 2nd Colleen
Fitzgerald mystery.   ISBN 1-56280-211-9   11.95

RIVER QUAY by Janet McClellan. 208 pp. 3rd Tru North
mystery.   ISBN 1-56280-212-7   11.95

ENDLESS LOVE by Lisa Shapiro. 272 pp. To believe, once
again, that love can be forever.   ISBN 1-56280-213-5   11.95

FALLEN FROM GRACE by Pat Welch. 256 pp. 6th Helen Black
mystery.   ISBN 1-56280-209-7   11.95

THE NAKED EYE by Catherine Ennis. 208 pp. Her lover in the
camera's eye . . .   ISBN 1-56280-210-0   11.95

OVER THE LINE by Tracey Richardson. 176 pp. 2nd Stevie
Houston mystery.   ISBN 1-56280-202-X   11.95

JULIA'S SONG by Ann O'Leary. 208 pp. Strangely
disturbing . . . strangely exciting.   ISBN 1-56280-197-X   11.95

LOVE IN THE BALANCE by Marianne K. Martin. 256 pp.
Weighing the costs of love . . .   ISBN 1-56280-199-6   11.95

PIECE OF MY HEART by Julia Watts. 208 pp. All the
stuff that dreams are made of —   ISBN 1-56280-206-2   11.95

MAKING UP FOR LOST TIME by Karin Kallmaker. 240 pp.
Nobody does it better . . .   ISBN 1-56280-196-1   11.95

GOLD FEVER by Lyn Denison. 224 pp. By author of *Dream
Lover*.   ISBN 1-56280-201-1   11.95

These are just a few of the many Naiad Press titles — we are the oldest and
largest lesbian/feminist publishing company in the world. We also offer an
enormous selection of lesbian video products. Please request a complete
catalog. We offer personal service; we encourage and welcome direct mail
orders from individuals who have limited access to bookstores carrying our
publications.